A LOVE LIKE STONE: A GARGOYLE STORY

LEXXY Q

TEXT UCP TO 22828 TO SUBSCRIBE TO OUR MAILING LIST
If you would like to join our team, submit the first 3-4 chapters of your completed manuscript to
Submissions@UrbanChapterspublications.com

To the me that always knew I could do this, and to the future me...if you ever forget...come back to this book and read it for yourself...you did it.

There may be terms that are unfamiliar in this book due to the nature of the magical scenes and dialog, so I've created a key for some of the words that you may need to remember or may not know 😊

Runes-tattoos or special markings that give power, strength, and release energy when tapped into.

Realm- the magical land of gargoyles and all things supernatural.

Shaman-magic man, wizard, sorcerer, someone with great power.

Akin-the same or alike.

The Scovel, Rose, and Ewing clans were named after real streets in Louisville and Nashville, after the places I was raised.

INTRODUCTION

In the Beginning....
AD

Before man was born, there were gargoyles created in the likeness of stone, meant to ward off evil spirits from homes, churches, and buildings alike for the upcoming human race. But one day, the need arose for a magical savior to reign over the majestic realms. A shaman, mighty in power, conjured up the greatest spell he could and infused it with love, the human race, and several other species to form something almost indestructible, like rock...the gargoyles...

The doors of the main chamber of King Kairo and Queen Zaya hurriedly shut behind them, where they escaped the many eyes of the kingdom. The first war between the humans and the gargoyles had finally broken out, after many years of trying to keep their secret. Several poor decisions led to their exposure, leaving them vulnerable to the one thing that can truly kill a gargoyle...steel. With their steel swords, knives, and even boulders, they'd found a way to wreak havoc on a once peaceful people.

Queen Zaya ignorantly believed if her people mated with the humans, this would help to restore the balance of the once magical creatures and bring forth a legacy that would forever allow the gargoyles to reign over any city, in any land, magical or not, but she was wrong. When she sent her best warriors to mate with the humans, she never foresaw the deadly consequences it would have. The babies were born as full men, or with tribal tattoos, fangs sharp as claws, or wings attached to their small bodies. This made the humans realize before it was time that their children were not born of this world. In an effort to contain the problem, Queen Zaya had their magical shaman place a protective barrier over their land, never to be seen by the humans, but by the time the shield went up, it was far too late; the humans had already penetrated the inside, and the war had begun.

To anyone looking in, King Kairo and Queen Zaya's relationship was one to TRULY envy. They were madly in love, though a mixed breed themselves, as no gargoyle had ever been pure in nature as of yet. They couldn't have been better suited for one another. Queen Zaya was left barren after a rape attack as a young gargoyle/ fairy breed. Without an heir to rule their kingdom in the event that something happened to one of the royals, the gargoyle race would surely die or be left to the hands of the wrong clan--even the humans.

The doors shut, and King Kairo and Queen Zaya were shut inside with their magical shaman, who was the last defense. His barrier had already been an epic fail, but he had one last move, one last thing that could potentially save them all.

"Jonas, what will we do? The kingdom will surely fall if we can't find a champion strong enough to overthrow the humans and the other clans. They've joined the humans to ruin our kingdom, what can be done?" Queen Zaya asked as she whipped her purple and gold robe behind her back and anxiously paced the floor of their bedchamber. "Calm down, my love, as always, we will defeat whoever has come against us, at any costs. I just wish..."

Queen Zaya glared at her husband. She couldn't stand to hear him say it one more time. She'd kept the truth from him about why she wasn't able to produce an heir for fear of him realizing she wasn't a virgin when they first united, not that it was her fault. She didn't willingly give her virginity away, it was stolen from her, just as her kingdom was about to be on this night.

"Do not worry, my king and queen. I have studied all of the books, magical and human akin. I know what we must do, but it will not be without pain or loss."

"Whatever it is, we have to do it. At this point, we're losing a war that seems to be never-ending. This is day five of the fight, and we've already lost so many. Their lives will not be lost in vain!" King Kairo shouted, vibrating the floor beneath him with his sharp words.

"I agree, my King. Up until this moment, there has never been a pure gargoyle created. Even you, Queen Zaya, are half fairy, and you, King Kairo, are half shape-shifter, the first of your kind born through love and magic. What we have been missing all this time was a magical creature to be CREATED, not born. King Kairo and Queen Zaya, it will take the most important parts of you if we are to succeed, and I will do the rest."

King Kairo approached his beautiful queen and looked into her eyes. He placed his hand upon her cheek, brushing it lightly with his thumb, reading her face for her agreement. Though he was the King, he loved his woman and appreciated her not because of her duty but because of her love for him. It was for that reason that he would never tell her what needed to be done, but instead, wait for her insight on the matter, and go from there.

Queen Zaya nodded her head, agreeing that whatever the shaman had in place would have to be for the better. After all, what more could they do if not this than to save at least the future race of gargoyles, even if they couldn't save them now.

"Splendid. My King, I'll need your rib, as all creation came from such, and your strength rune, as it is the first and like no other. It will grow back, of course."

King Kairo nodded and stood still, waiting for what was to come next. The shaman approached him and placed his hand on his rib, calling it forth with the magic inside him. Though no words were spoken, the king and queen could feel the presence of his magic working in their favor.

"Shit!" Kairo yelled as he felt his bone breaking from his body, pushing its way through his flesh. The thought of losing a rib didn't initially seem like it would hurt too bad, seeing as how he'd broken many bones as a young prince, but this, this felt like death.

"I apologize, my king. As I said, it will not be without pain or loss."

"Continue, hurry!"

The shaman continued calling the rib forth. Once it was completely out of his body, he put it on the silver decorated plate that would now serve as an altar for their magical concoction. He replaced the open wound with his hand, and it was as it was before, closed and unwounded. King Kairo held out his arm, where his strength rune was. The rune was gifted from the first shaman for his courageous efforts to save his family many years ago. The rune was used to draw energy upon whenever he felt weak. He glanced down at it, wondering how long it would take to get back. This would hurt worse than him losing a rib, as it would be an emotional pain, not so much physical. The shaman took out his sacrificial knife and began carving it into the king's arm, releasing his rune from his body. For a moment, weakness swept over

Kairo's heart and mind, reminding him of what he was like before he became king when he was just a boy.

"You are strong even without the rune, my love. For it is only a mark, one that will grow back. Your strength, your true strength, lies inside of you, with your heart, and your love." Queen Zaya comforted the king, reminding him of what was most important.

A smile crept upon his face as he viewed his beautiful wife. She was his, and he was hers, and together, they knew they could defeat the enemy.

"Now, it is your turn, my queen. Step forward please," Jonas said as he raised his hand to meet her forehead.

"From you, I will extract knowledge, love from your soul, as that is how you truly love, and part of your womb, for protection, as the womb is the safest place any man or woman could ever be."

Worry washed over Queen Zaya. She'd never told anyone about her damaged and bruised uterus. Surely it would not protect the creature to come. In an effort to free herself from guilt in case this did not work, she began to speak.

"Kairo, I need to tell you something. My womb— "

"My darling, I know everything about you there is to know. Just because your womb could not house a seed of our own, doesn't mean that it cannot magically sustain another. I know what happened to you as a young girl, and that is why I've banished the fairies from ever returning to our realm. It was the way of their people, to rape and plunder. I know you were born in rape and were raped yourself, but I see you no differently, and I love you no differently."

This was the first time she'd ever heard him say it. She assumed he didn't know because it was a secret she vowed to take to her grave. She knew about her lineage and how she'd come from a violent past, but she never expected her husband of all people to know the truth, especially when she'd done everything she could to keep it hidden.

Tears released from her eyes, tumbling down like tumbleweeds, falling onto her royal robes. "You are beautiful, you are mine, and you are not without worth, my queen." For the first time, King Kairo bowed to his queen, as she was just as much royalty as he was himself.

The shaman continued with the ritual, bringing forth the queen's knowledge, love from her soul, and her womb to protect the creature to be, and emptied their essence into the mixing plate on the altar. Though he had not mentioned it, he included a piece of steel as to make him immune to the attacks from the humans, but he wasn't quite sure if it would work. He had faith that it would at least work for a while.

"Step back," Jonas announced as he began wafting his hands over the altar, saying a sacred spell that he was practically winging, speaking from his spirit and not his mind.

After he'd done all he could do, preparing the ingredients and blessing them, a purple smoke and haze formed around the plate, producing a very large egg that was cracking at the seams.

Queen Zaya and King Kairo looked on in horror and amazement as the egg finally popped open and produced what they would believe to be a god, their champion.

From the egg spurned a chocolate, ab riddled, bearded, tattooed man, carrying the strength rune of the king and even the queen's essence seemed to be dripping off of him.

As he got his footing, stone-like wings emerged from his naked body, covering his manly tool and enclosing him in a cocoon as he kneeled before the king and queen.

"How may I serve you?" he asked as he got to his knees.

"First, someone get this man some clothes. I don't want to see all of that," the king said, clearly not wanting to see a naked man in his presence, or have one be in front of his wife.

Jonas took off his red robe and draped it over the man's brilliantly large wings.

"I think we should call him Stone, as he will be the rock that holds our world together," Queen Zaya announced, and her king couldn't have agreed more.

"Rise, young warrior. Jonas, open the curtains, let him see with his eyes."

Jonas obliged the queen and opened the curtains of their bedroom, where down below, Stone could see the mayhem that had befallen the people. There was blood everywhere, drenching the palace, humans and gargoyles alike had been slayed, meeting their untimely deaths.

"You, Stone, are our champion, created from us and magic, as the first, pure gargoyle to save our kingdom. Jonas, is he immortal?" Queen Zaya shifted her head to Jonas' direction, wondering why that wasn't something they'd previously talked about.

"Nothing is truly immortal, but he should be able to withstand most if not all of the hits the humans or other gargoyles may unleash."

"Wonderful! Stone, go forth and protect what is ours, and I promise, there will always be a place for you in our kingdom." The king placed his hands on his shoulders, and almost instinctively, Stone felt his wings fluttering, and then, lift him off the ground, thrusting him down into the fight.

From above, the king, queen, and Jonas could see everything moving, and Stone was quite impressive. His first victim was picked up by the talons from his feet, something none of them had noticed when he was in the room with them, and slung to the other side of the moat, which was at least thirty feet. The next rushed him with a steel sword, and this would be the true test. Stone grabbed the sword, holding it tightly in his hand, scaring the human in front of him, as he'd never seen anything like it. He believed all gargoyles could be killed by steel, but not Stone; he was different from the rest. Under his grip, the blade crumbled and disintegrated, leaving only ashes behind.

As Stone went on, he, along with his fellow gargoyle brethren defeated the humans and the rival clan, making them victorious once again over their land. Jonas, seeing the victory afoot, placed the barrier up, finally to keep the humans out for good, and peace fell upon the kingdom.

Stone, proud of himself, yet still a bit confused, flew to the top of the palace, sitting on its highest peak, resting and watching to see what would happen next.

The king and queen appeared upon their balcony, where their subjects below applauded and cheered, as their kingdom had been saved, and the war was over.

"My sons and daughters, you have fought bravely on this night, along with the many others in which we have defeated our enemy, but this, the wasteland of bodies you see before you, are only a prelude to what will come. Though this was the first war many of you have seen, this will not be the last, as we now have clan members who would turn against us, to overthrow the kingdom for their power, but I vow, on this night, that with our champion Stone, and the likes of all of you, we will face what is to come TOGETHER!" King Kairo proudly announced, his words reaching the entire kingdom.

Their loyal subjects bowed down, allowing their wings to wrap them up in honor of their king and queen, and though no one would dare say it, their savior, Stone.

On his peak, before the sun rose, his eyes glowed a shimmering silver, where he would watch over the kingdom for the rest of his days...

🦎 I 🦎
PRESENT DAY STONE

As the year's progress, it seems as though no matter how much time passes, nothing ever truly changes. It's been six centuries since our last full on out war. We've had many battles since then, but nothing that couldn't be contained, until now. The clan Ewing, the clan I was proud to be a part of, was constantly falling victim to fuck shit. I mean, I have never in my life, and I've been alive a long time, witnessed such turmoil between what should be families, but power, greed, and lack of wealth will turn anyone cold and make them do things they wouldn't otherwise do.

As the first pure gargoyle, I'd done everything in my power to fight against the many threats that came against my family as often as I could, but I am but one person and can only do so much. The long, unclear history of the gargoyles seemed to be one that was lost throughout the ages, where the stories were misconstrued and somehow got screwed up. So, here's the truth: gargoyles love hard, protect harder, and we are some of the most loyal muthafuckas there are. I can't call us people, even though some of us are, but hardly any are anymore, especially since we've been banned from consorting with humans, but we're hardly human, but have so many human emotions. The human and gargoyle worlds couldn't be more alike, and that was true.

From the lack of knowledge and foolishness of many of our clan and humans and consorting with our enemy clans, such as the Rose clan, the Scovel clan, and the Scott clan, once again, we were in a damn battle for our lives, well, their lives. I was practically immortal, which was the worst part because I'd had to see so many others before me die, or worse, be turned to stone and never to turn back. Contrary to popular belief, gargoyles were not meant to be stone objects, but after a curse was placed on the clans in the fourteenth century because of all the fighting, by an evil shaman, gargoyles, outside of the realm, were now forced to be turned into stone from dusk till dawn, only to move about the human world during the night, which was stupid as fuck to me, so that warding off evil spirits shit is dead. The reason we look so damn ugly at the moment, I mean, you imagine being turned into stone, it is not fucking fun, and the shit hurts like a bitch. You'd make an ugly ass face too if you were stuck up on a building where you can't be disturbed for hours on end, knowing your joints and shit gon' be achin' when you get back up. That's another reason why gargoyles are so fucking strong. We gotta be to handle the transformation our bodies go through. Even I'm not exempt from the curse, that's one of many things that sucked about being created. Even though I wasn't born, I still had to suffer through many of the same things the others did, like turning into stone the moment I set foot into the human world, where many of the clans, against our natural order, were hiding out in secret, pretending to be human, or being assigned a mate, a "true" mate, whatever the fuck that was.

I was supposed to feel from the moment I met her that we were destined to be together. That somehow the earth beneath my magical ass feet would shift and draw me to her, but that hadn't happened yet. I've honestly been waiting at least fifty years for it too. My "true" mate Pandora, though beautiful, was not for me. Her hair was dreaded up and beaded with our tribal symbols, and she had even more runes than I did. She was much younger than I was, but age is relative as a practically immortal being. She was one of the strongest women in the Ewing clan, and I should have been happy to have her, but I wasn't, and I didn't want her. She was smart and beautiful but wound very tightly. She didn't know how to let loose and enjoy her life, but that doesn't mean every now, and then I didn't like sleeping with her. Sleeping with Pandora was very, very rare, but it was unacceptable for me to sleep with the other women in our clan, considering King Kairo and Queen Zaya named her my true mate long ago. Though the women would flirt with me, none of them would ever cross that line. Nor would I, because I believed in my calling and my purpose. Above my duty, I'd grown to love, and care about the king and queen, I hoped one day I would be able to feel this bond that Pandora and I were supposed to share. She claimed she could feel it, but I was still lost on how, because I couldn't figure it out. Even as I lay here beside her, I was still confused. Sex, to my understanding, was supposed to bring you closer, but for some reason, I just knew there had to be more out there for me, I didn't know where.

Lying next to Pandora, I never felt settled, but especially not tonight. Something just didn't seem right. My heartfelt off like something was nudging me out of bed, so I had to listen to it. I slid out of bed, not caring if I woke up Pandora, which I eventually did, and grabbed my gray sweatpants from the floor, placing my legs inside.

"Mmm...Stone, what are you doing? Come back to bed," Pandora moaned as she awakened.

"Nah, I'll be back, something isn't right."

Like a dog, her ears went up and became more alert. One thing I could say about Pandora was she was with the shit. If there was ever something going on, beside me, she was right there. She always had my back, and for that, I would always have love for her, just not in that way.

"I'm going too."

Before I could say a word, she was already out of bed, throwing on her shorts and a t-shirt. Don't look so surprised, we got human bodies that need to be covered up. All the glory we were bestowed with could knock somebody the fuck out, trust.

I wasn't even going to argue with her because we could ruin a whole kingdom that way, we'd almost done it before not even ten years ago, and I wasn't trying to do that again.

I ripped the door open jogging down the hallway toward the king and queen's room; my intuition just led me there. I felt like I had to be there like that was where I was needed. Of course, Pandora was right beside my ass as always. Approaching their door, it was wide open, and the guards were standing inside looking as confused as they possibly could.

"What happened? Where's Kairo and Zaya?" I asked, looking up at the clock in their room. It was after one a.m., where could they be at this hour?

"Champion, I'm glad you're here, I'll speak with you and Pandora, privately," Jonas said as he tilted his glasses down his face, letting the guards know they needed to get out of the room. Though Jonas was old as dirt now, he was still hanging on. He was still just as quick with the magic as he had always been.

When the guards fled the room, Pandora looked around and then out the window, I guess she could sense the danger I was also feeling now, not knowing where the king and queen were.

"Stone, you have to go into the human world. Zaya and Kairo have been off on one of their peace missions, alone. I just got word myself that this is where they ran off to not thirty minutes ago. They told me they were going for a walk through the garden and then to enjoy a date, I had no idea this "date" would be a suicide mission."

Anger pulsated through my body, and I could feel the runes on my arms beginning to warm up. I reached for Jonas' throat, throwing him up against the wall, choking him to what could be his death if he didn't give me answers.

"And why did they go alone? Seriously, no fucking guards? Nah, this sounds like a fucking set up. Why didn't someone come and get me?" I asked through gritted teeth.

"Who would dare let them set foot outside of the fucking kingdom? I'm not understanding. Where are they? Who did they try and make peace with? Please, for the love of all things gargoyle don't tell me them fuckin' Rose's or the damn Scovels."

Jonas was clawing at my hand, and I could feel Pandora's eyes beaming into my back. If I wanted any answers, I would have to put Jonas down so he could answer the questions properly.

Taking a deep breath, he grasped at his throat, almost like he could still feel my hands around them and said "You're right, they shouldn't have gone alone, not even on some stupid date, but they're almost a millennium old, they know better, but you have to go and get them. They're with the Scovels."

I threw my hands up in frustration, and there wasn't enough time for me to do anything but react. I ran back to the suite I shared with Pandora and put on a shirt, tennis shoes, and grabbed my weapons to head out into the human world. It was hunting time.

Pandora was on my heels as I left out of the room. She

had her shoes in hand. I figured she'd put them on when she got a chance.

"Where are your weapons?" I asked her, looking at how she carried nothing but her shoes.

"Don't need 'em, I've got these, remember?" Pandora held her hand up, her claws at full length and ready to fuck something up.

"Nah, I ain't forget...come on."

I can't lie, that shit turned me on like a muthafucka! Having sex with Pandora was good, and sometimes, it got freaky as hell, but there was nothing there. I didn't feel that gravitational pull, and I felt like I should. I didn't feel her in my spirit in the moment. The fucked-up thing though, was because she was supposedly my true mate, I could feel her inside of me, like when we were away from each other. I could almost hear her thoughts I could feel her feelings so strongly. That shit was beyond annoying. When she was horny, it would burn me alive until I fucked her. If she was sick, I would feel weak as fuck when I wasn't with her, and that shit was the worst. I remember when she had a little stomach bug not too long ago, I wanted to kill her dead because I couldn't stay off the toilet. What? Y'all thought we couldn't get sick? Shit, we get sick too. Maybe not as bad, but it does happen. The older we get, the more the magic inside of us fades, which is what makes us so strong in the first place.

She retracted her claws as we left the palace. We tried to keep as low of a profile as possible and tried to keep our heads down. No one needed to know that for whatever reason, the king and queen thought it was a bright idea to go out on their own, knowing it wasn't, and that it would cause major problems. When I saw them, I would let them know. Though they may not have known it, I considered them my parents. They were good to me and had practically "raised" me as their own. In this moment, I felt weaker than I'd ever been. I was strong and courageous, yes. I had the muscle, the brawn, the dick size that said I'm that gargoyle, but in this moment, I wasn't feeling that. If something happened to them, the kingdom would never be the same. Both of them were irreplaceable. Though there was, of course, other tribes ready to come to the forefront and take over, the way the gargoyle nation was ruled would be different; corrupt, overrun with bullshit, and our traditions, the few we had left, would be washed away and forgotten. I couldn't let that happen.

Though I tried to make it seem like we weren't in a hurry, the closer we got to the perimeter of the realm, Pandora and I picked up our speed from a brisk walk to a full on outrun. It would take that much energy anyway to break through the magical barrier. Shit, I don't know why anyone would want to leave any damn way. It almost hurt to get out of this magical ass shit, but see, Jonas made it that way after the gargoyles were cursed with turning into stone involuntarily, so that we would want to stay inside where we were safe, but that didn't stop some of us from going out. If it were up to me, I would never leave; I had no reason to. Every now and then, I had to go out to make sure the other clans were staying in order and staying out of the way, which was hardly ever, but for the most part, they brought the noise to us. Right here, on our turf, so I wasn't as familiar with the human world as I could have been, not as much as Queen Zaya and King Kairo.

As we ran through the barrier, we came out on the other side into an alley.

"Where are we?" Pandora asked as she looked around, covering her nose and mouth with her shirt. "It smells terrible here, Stone. Damn!" "Shh...I can't concentrate. I need to focus so I can see."

"Fine, fine!" Pandora threw up her hands and backed up

against the wall of the alley. She already knew what I was about to do. One of the best parts about being a gargoyle was the sight. We were meant to protect and to see the attack before it happened, so my sight was so out of this world, not only could I see what was happening, up to a certain distance, I could see what had happened. All I had to do was touch something. The building beside me was radiating with heat signatures of that of our world, so I figured someone of our kind had to have been here. I placed my hand on the building, and like a movie, the scene flashed into my mind. It was as if I were there with them.

I could see the humans who were getting high in the alleyway just before the king and queen appeared, but then they fled and took off. It was too cold for them to stay here with the air flapping and smacking them in the face. They appeared to be homeless as well. After they were gone, the king and queen stepped through the barrier. I could smell their scent it was so strong. The smell of lavender and honey invaded my nostrils. I sniffed the air, using my ole factory senses to guide me. As I walked along the wall, I could see them; they had worried looks on their faces, but Kairo was trying to keep Zaya calm. He had his hand around her shoulder, and she had her head caught in between his neck as if she was in need of comfort.

I followed the building until I couldn't anymore, and let my senses do the rest. Behind me, I could hear Pandora's feet mimicking my steps, paying mind to stay close behind me. It was like being in two worlds at once—the world that I was walking in and the world that was here before I was. Past and present type shit. Across the street, I continued on the path that would hopefully lead to the king and queen.

"Stone, watch out!" Pandora snatched me backwards, breaking me from my concentration. "Pandora, what the fuck are you doing?" "Yeah, yell at me, fool. You almost walked right into the damn street. I'm so sorry for saving your life. Fuck outta here."

I turned around and stared into her eyes. Pandora and I used to fight one another all the time, but it had been a long time since I put my hands on her, If she didn't watch it tonight, we were going to have a fucking reoccurrence. I stepped toward her, but then decided against it. We had more pressing issues to tend to than me stomping her ass out in the middle of the road. "Just come on." I rolled my eyes and stood there, trying to get back in tune with my senses so I could find the king and queen and get us all home.

I continued following the trail I had before Pandora inter-rupted me, hoping I'd pick back up the vibe I had before about the direction. Then it hit me, I could see their heat signatures against the building ahead, along with the vision of them, so I had no choice but to follow it. I stepped out into the middle of the street, following what I knew would lead us to them. The city of Louisville never slept. It was always live, especially on Bardstown road, where we were, but it was getting late, so hopefully the humans would be going in soon like we needed them to. The time was beginning to get to my body the closer it got to sunrise. We only had three hours before the sun began to peek, and we needed to be back in our world before then, or we'd spend the day up on someone's building in stone.

The trail led on for about two miles, and finally, with Pandora bumping into my back, we ran into a building that held the gargoyle runes. A human wouldn't be able to see the runes. You'd have to be gargoyle to see them, but they were as clear as day to me.

"We're here," I said, rubbing my hand over the runes, taking them all in. Once upon a time, the clans were united. I had never seen that time period. All I knew was war, but I could only imagine how peaceful it might have been before I was created. I was brought about in a place of stress and unrest, and if the clans could join together to stop fighting, the gargoyle race wouldn't be dying out, whether it was pure or not.

Pandora came to the left side of me, standing, waiting for my orders. I didn't knock; there was no point. For all I knew, they could be holding the king and queen hostage. If they were, even though we would be outnumbered, they would have one hell of a fight to put up with, with me and Pandora. If we needed help, hopefully, someone would be back in the realm paying attention to the vibes we were letting off, but those damn gargoyles were hardheaded and had their agendas. They wouldn't know how to stand together, really stand together if their lives depended on it, and it did, but they were too stupid to realize it.

The quieter my mind became, I realized there was music playing, loud music coming from inside the building. Then I looked on top of the rune, and it said, Bar Scovel. These gargoyles had a bar that they were running to use as a cover in the human world. That shit was smart as fuck, but definitely against the rules. I couldn't figure out why the king and queen would dare come here. As if Pandora was picking up on the same thing I was, she shook her head and looked at me.

"Ion know why you lookin' at me. We goin' in, and I don't know what to expect on the other side, so be ready for anything."

"I was born ready, literally." Pandora released her claws once more, ready for whatever might be waiting for us on the other side of the door.

I pushed it open and walked straight in, chest out, ready to get down if need be. Almost as if on cue, the music stopped, and everyone looked in our direction. I recognized some of these fools, specifically the leader of the Scovel clan, Black. Me and this dude have had problems almost since the day I was created. I defeated their clan back in 1250 AD, and we'd been having problems since then. Every time some shit popped off, it was always because of him. See, he was one of those dudes that had a light-skinned gargoyle complex. Yeah, that shit is real as fuck even in our community. He thought he was the best looking, the smartest, the best leader, the one to change some shit, but he was going about it all wrong. True, peaceful protest doesn't always get the job done, but neither does fighting all the damn time, and that was all he knew how to do. I have to give it to dude; his battle strategies were beastly. He could unleash a sneak attack on you, and you would NEVER see it coming, another reason, why now stepping into this bar, I felt nervous. For all I knew, they could be trying to ambush us here, or in the realm. They could have the king and queen held against their will. Then, I started wonder who the hell gave Jonas word that this shit was going on anyway? I hoped he wasn't on some disloyal shit. Kairo and Zaya had been good to him, and for real, he was like an uncle to me, if that was a thing in our world, since we were all like brother and sister, or mother and daughter. The terminology don't matter, but it would be a terrible feeling and loss to have to go through some shit like that if Jonas wasn't living his best life the right way.

Black was standing behind the bar; it seemed as if there were only gargoyles in the joint tonight, I could sense the magic in all of them. "Uhm, look what the magic drug in. How can we help you, Rock?"

"Gargoyle don't act like you don't know my name. Where are the king and the queen?"

"Seems like to me, you think you gon' come in my bar, making noise, actin' like you run shit in here when that ain't the case. You want answers, you ask nicely. I know you see all these men around you ready to take you out. We don't fuck with your kind around here."

"What kind is that? The pure, real kind? Must be what you talkin' 'bout because from what I'm looking around and seeing, y'all look like a bunch of half-bloods to me."

As soon as I said it, I regretted it, because Pandora was a half breed too, and I didn't want her to feel like I was also throwing a shot at her lineage, because that wasn't what I was doing. I looked over to her, and she had a smile on her face.

"Shit don't bother me. They're the ones that act like half-breeds, I don't," she said tucking her dreads behind her ears. She was one of the only women I had ever seen a fight with her hair down. She never tied that shit up. I think that shit turned her on because in the many battles we'd fought in together, I could feel the sexual arousal jumping off her body.

"Who you callin' half-breed, bitch?" Black asked as he hopped from behind the bar, his knees touching his chest with precision. I moved to stand in front of Pandora, because at the end of the day, she was a woman, whether she could protect herself or not.

"Woah, Woah, you need to chill with all of that Black. We came here for Kairo and Zaya; once we get them, we'll be out of your hair, so what you wanna do?"

Pandora was behind me huffing and puffing, acting like she was going to blow the damn bar down, and I wouldn't be surprised with the morning breath that she now had if she couldn't.

Black looked around me to Pandora and licked his lips, and it didn't bother me one bit. This was another reason I knew I didn't give a damn about Pandora being my true mate. How could she be my true mate anyway, when she was selected for me based on our likeness and how close we should have been? I didn't give a damn though; I knew she wasn't for me. If I did care, I would've been jealous or feeling protective over her for another man trying her, but I wasn't feeling any type of way about it. Hell, he could have her if he wanted her. It wasn't like she wasn't on the market, because she was, whether she was willing to admit it to herself or not. I felt bad because we kept on having sex, even though I wasn't in love with her. A gargoyle was about to lose his damn mind not being able to bust a nut off with another woman, so it had to be like this.

"Shit, you know what, you came into my bar, asking for something in my, what you could call, house, so what you got to offer? Perhaps you're finally ready to get them hands up and have that fight we've been itchin' at for the last three hundred years."

"My gargoyle, you still trippin' about somethin' that happened three-hundred years ago? Sounds like to me you need to get a life, but if that's the only thing that will get the king and queen out here and back in the realm, then I'll do it."

"Stone, don't do this. This is what he wants. What if it's a trap?" Pandora whispered into my ear from behind me. I turned around to face her, seeing the worry and concern all over her face. "Even if it is a trap, oh well. If you sense some bull shit while I'm in the thick of it, find your way out of here and take the king and the queen with you."

"As a matter of fact, before I agree, I want to see them to make sure they're alive and in good health." Black looked at me, his eyes began glowing a reddish brown, and he let out a loud growl before walking away and opening up the door behind the bar.

"Come on this way, then, but after this, you better be ready. I've been waiting on this a long time." I nodded my head and pulled Pandora in front of me. If for some reason this was a trap, and they tried to attack from behind, I wanted her to have the upper hand of being in the middle, so she could take care of herself. We followed Black to the room, and on the inside, it seemed as if the room was set up to be some sort of office. I had to admit, my gargoyle brothers were up on everything. Even business and that was why it was a damn shame we couldn't all keep it together.

The further we got into the office, behind the desk, on the floor, Kairo and Zaya were sitting up against the wall. They weren't tied up, but still sitting there.

"Kairo, Zaya..." I quickly fell to my knees and bowed. "Are you alright? Is everything ok?" I began panicking. Though I was one of the hardest warriors around, I had a heart, and I loved my king and queen and wanted to make sure they were ok.

"We're doing just fine, Stone. Don't worry." "Don't worry? You're back here doing what, exactly? You're not tied up, why are you all staying back here?"

Zaya's face confused me. I didn't understand; if they weren't being held here against their will, what were they doing here? "Answer me!" I roared with anger.

"We decided to make a trade. The clans have been warring entirely too long, and as king and queen over not just the realm, but as gargoyles, it is our job to do all we can to make peace for the future generations. No matter how many futures ahead of us that will be."

"What kind of trade, your majesty?" Pandora asked Kairo as she stepped forward, joining me on her knees as well. "Will the two of you get up? Listen, sometimes, as rulers, you have to figure out what works best for the kingdom. What works best, or will work best now, is giving up the throne and letting someone else rule. Believe it or not, the Scovel clan hasn't always been bad, not really. They're just misguided and need some leadership, and they will have that, in Black. He will lead the new king and queen-elect after we officially step down."

"Wait one fuckin' minute," I said as I rose to my feet. "Ain't no way in gargoyle hell, I'ma let you do some shit like this. How could you do this? You weren't even going to tell anybody. You weren't going to tell me, your champion? I'm like your fucking son, how could you do this? If you're stepping down, the fuck you doing here, then?"

"Stone, calm down, are you crazy? They're still the king and queen." Pandora spun off her knees and back onto her feet, trying to embrace me, but I, of course, pushed her away.

"Nah, I'm not gonna calm down. Do you hear them, do you hear what they're saying?" "Stone, that's enough!" Kairo's voice almost broke the office around us. The walls trembled as his voice was like a sonic boom being released throughout the bar. "You will still give the respect you rightfully know to give, as the circumstances may seem unorthodox, I frankly don't give a damn. Stand down, Stone, this is the way it must and will be."

I threw my hands up not knowing what else to say. How could they be willing to give up so easily, and almost as if Pandora could read my mind, she said, "They've been at it for centuries. Maybe they are tired, Stone."

I couldn't believe her. Whose side was she on? Was I the only one seeing reason? I didn't want to say anything, but I felt the heart that beat along with Zaya's tearing like it was breaking. I looked down at my feet to keep myself from showing the obvious tears that were about to fall. Then, Zaya came over to me and pulled me into her warm, queenly embrace, holding me like only a mother could.

"Stone, you don't see how this is a good thing right now, but I promise you, this is the only way. Unfortunately, ruling is not as fun and as easy as it may appear to be. It calls for us to sacrifice and make decisions that our subjects and families may not understand, but this must be done. Now, whether you're willing to go with it or not, this will happen, so it's best that you fall in line. You were created to save us, and I believe you still will, even if it isn't in battle. Perhaps you will be the stone that keeps the Ewing clan together."

"Alright, I let y'all have your minute to make sure they were alright. Now, bring ya' ass on up out of here, and let's get to it!" Black interrupted the moment I was having with Queen Zaya, but a deal was a deal. Besides that, I was straight up plotting on this nigga anyway. I gave Zaya and Kairo a longing look, and they both smiled, knowing I could handle this dude with my eyes closed, but to prove a point to himself, he was willing to get himself killed.

"You comin'?" I asked Pandora as she shook her head. "Wherever you go, I'll go." Pandora was loyal as fuck, and I hated it, only because I couldn't give her what she wanted, my love in return.

We headed out of the office, and back in the bar, the Scovel clan was cheering and chanting Black's name, hyping him up. He clearly needed it. I'm a movement by myself, I don't need the fuckin' hype, but I'd let him have it. Maybe it would give him some type of secret strength.

Black took off his V-neck white t-shirt, a shirt that only little boys wear, nigga couldn't even put on a regular t-shirt, and tightened his belt on his jeans. I only had on my t-shirt and sweatpants, and I didn't give a damn about getting blood on it since I knew it wouldn't be mine.

We met in the middle of the room, where the

Scovel clan gathered around us in a circle, acting like we were about to have a dance fight or some shit I'd seen on TV. Yeah, we got that shit too. Don't be fooled, technology is good for everyone, even magical creatures.

Pandora joined me, standing behind me, watching and waiting to see who would make the first move, which it wouldn't be me. He wanted this damn fight, he'd have to come at me.

"Come at me then, Scovel. This what you wanted, right?"

"Since forever...aggghhhh!" Black yelled, releasing his giant black wings, the reason he got the name Black. He was the only gargoyle known to have those black wings. Most of our wings were gray, sometimes white, hell sometimes a mixture of both, but never black, which made me feel like that gargoyle was pure evil. His eyes burned that reddish-brown as they had before, and I knew he was about to come at me full force, or what he considered to be so.

He flew at me. Literally, his chest bumping up against mine. I waited until he got close enough, and then I grabbed him, releasing my talons into his wings. His flesh swelled around my fingertips.

"Ha-ha, is that all you got?"

Black began flapping his wings, flying us into the wall of the bar where there were liquor bottles and glasses that were now shattered and scattered along the floor.

I pulled one of my hands out of his wings and pulled back, sending my fist flying into his right cheek. Blood and spit spewed out of his mouth, hitting my shirt and on the floor, causing him to drop me.

My feet hit the ground, and I jumped onto the bar, waiting for his next move. Soon after, he joined me, standing in front of me. From there, our hands were perfectly in sync as the hand-to-hand combat commenced. He was quick, I had to give it to him, and his hands were nice, but nowhere near mine. I didn't have to fight dirty to get his ass. He raised his leg and kicked me in the knees. I ain't gon' lie, that shit felt like his foot was fucking rock.

"Shit!" I screamed as my legs buckled, bringing me down to my knees. Then, suddenly, I felt something inside of me, something strange. Something was happening. As the other gargoyles were chanting and still cheering and getting closer, something else was happening.

I turned around to see Pandora slowly fleeing the bar,

with the king and queen ahead of her. Damn, that was one thing I couldn't deny—Pandora was on her shit. She was so in tune with me. It was stuff like this that made me wonder why we weren't clicking properly. She was a good match for me in every other way minus the personal shit. She just didn't know how to relax, how to have a good time, how to be a normal gargoyle, and I was tired of it. I just wanted her to loosen up a bit, but she always had my back, and right now, that was what we needed.

I had to do my best to keep everyone distracted, so if it was a fight they wanted, it was a fight they would get. I got up, using all the strength I had inside of me, and swung Black around and flipped him onto his back onto the bar. I put my foot on his throat, where he began flailing like a fish, flopping and bumping around. He reached up and squeezed my ankle, something that didn't faze me, and instead of looking to see if they'd made it out, I relied on my feelings and instincts, hoping they had made it.

"Now, what was all that shit you was talkin', Black? Three-hundred years done gone by since I last got up with you, and you still can't take me? Fucking tragic!" he was grabbing at my leg, squeezing as tightly as he could. I wouldn't kill him; it was against the law unless in battle, and this was far from fucking battle, but I clearly needed to remind him who the fuck I was and what was real.

"You done with this lil' shit? Huh, can I go the fuck on about my night?" He wasn't budging, and he didn't have one word to say. Well, maybe he did, but he was under my shoe, so there wasn't much he could say. I was done playing his game, so I jumped off the bar and onto the floor, looking around the crowd. Though some of them looked like they wanted to try me, they fucking knew better. They saw I whooped their clan leader up, and eventually, there would be a round two, but not tonight. As they should have, I was beginning to feel the pain in my body. The sun would be coming up soon, and we needed to be back in the realm before that happened. Damn, where did those hours go?

As I walked through the crowd, the Scovel clan growled at me, some of them scratching and clawing at me, but they wouldn't' dare take me, and I wasn't afraid. If they wanted it, they could get it, but I hoped I could get out in time.

When the door to the bar opened, I stepped out, no harm, no foul. There was no problem, and ahead of me, was Pandora, the king, and the queen, clearly waiting for me. A smile found my lips, and I began making my way over to them, but before I could get back into the alleyway good, I was forced to the ground, being knocked feet away from the bar. My body skidded a bit as it slid down the hard gravel.

"Uhn!" I grunted as my body thumped over and over. "Yeah, you thought this shit was over, but it ain't. You can't come into my bar doin' whatever you want, thinkin' I'ma let you have the upper hand."

"My gargoyle, you gotta let this go. You got an L, take that shit and go the fuck o—"

I couldn't finish my sentence, and Black's movements toward me completely stopped. We were both feeling the same thing—the sun.

"This ain't over yet, nigga!" After he said that, he turned his back and began running back in the bar, where the blinds were immediately shut, and something went over them because it was completely black. The sky was turning light, and it was time for us to get back to where we belonged. With the little bit of strength, I did have left, I rose to my feet and began limping. My knee still hurt from the blow he'd delivered to it, but I could make it to the portal in time, or so I hoped.

Limping, I moved as quickly as I could out of one alley to cross the street to get to the other side.

"Stone, you must hurry!" the queen anxiously said as she began trying to cross the street to get to me. Something in me began feeling sick. She was exposed, and if the sun completely rose on her in this moment, she'd be stone for sure.

I tried to run toward her and meet her halfway, but before I could, the sun completely rose, and I don't know, it all just happened so fast. We weren't going to make it back into the realm in enough time, but the top of the building wasn't too far away to reach to rest comfortably for the day, but for the first time ever, the sun rose faster than it ever had, and the queen immediately turned to stone. Pandora, I, and the king were already in the air, headed to the top of the building; it was too late.

As my body began turning to stone, I saw the worst sight I could have ever seen—a speeding car came down the road, smashing the now stone queen's body, never to be put back together. I turned my head, that was still mobile and looked at the king, who had his mouth open as if he were about to scream, and a lone tear escaped his eye but had stopped mid-cheek.

Though I knew the longer we stayed in the human world our magic faded, I had never seen it with my own two eyes. That would be the only explanation or reason that the queen couldn't make it out of the road. She sacrificed herself, whether she realized it or not, for me, and for that, I would never forgive myself. I would never be whole again. I single-handedly was the cause of her demise. I wondered how Pandora was even able to get them to come with her. With a broken heart that I could feel deep in my soul, I could feel exactly what she was feeling, we both turned into stone....

2

LUNA

"**G**ood morning, Luna, how are you feeling?" the doctor asked me as I rolled over onto my side. I felt numb, dead really, but a bitch can't say that to a doctor. That's how you end up in the fucking psych ward. The way I was feeling, shit, maybe that was where I needed to be, but not right now, not at all really. I was trippin'.

"I'm not sure. I'm still in a little pain. You think I could get some more of those pain meds?" Shit, if I was going to have to be in the hospital, I needed something to ease the way I was feeling on the inside and on the outside. The worst part about emotional pain was you couldn't sleep it off, you couldn't walk it off, and you damn sure couldn't talk it off. The only thing you could do was numb yourself and pray that one day that shit went away on its own.

Here I was laid up in the hospital, wishing I was dead, for real. I'd been here for two days, and I'd be going home today. Even though I felt like I should stay another day, shit, another week, I guess losing a baby doesn't call for a long hospital visit. A month ago, I was somewhat happy. I was pregnant, working, living in my rundown ass project, but I was happy because I had something to look forward to, someone to be better for.

It was too early to know if it was a boy or a girl, but that didn't matter to me as long as it was healthy. From what I knew, it was healthy, but I guess not because a few days ago, I started having pains in my lower abdomen, and I wanted to scream, as a matter of fact, I'm sure I did, but I didn't want to come to the hospital. To me, that would make it all too real, and I wasn't ready to deal with that shit, not yet. That is until I couldn't bear it any longer. I was hurting something terrible, literally, and I had to call 911. Once the operator got on the line, I began crying. My heart was broken because I already knew what was happening. I knew for sure what the problem was, and there was nothing I could do about it.

Blood sloshed down my jeans, and I couldn't even stand to my feet. When the EMT's came into my "apartment", that's what I call my project, I was so embarrassed. No matter how clean it was, it was never clean enough. They came in and began immediately assessing the situation. I told them I was pregnant, and they rushed me straight to the hospital, where my accusation of losing my baby was later confirmed. I was devastated, and most of all, I felt like an idiot and a failure.

I'd been messing around with this guy named

Link and I thought he was the damn bee's knees, but I couldn't have been more wrong. We'd been dealing with one another for a good two years before I found out that he was married with not one, not two, but three fucking baby mamas. I found out one night while going through his phone. Yep, I sure fucking did, and I would do it again if time was rewound. This was before I knew I was pregnant, but the moment I found out, he was gone. There was no way he could come back from all the lies he'd told me. The whole time I was messing with him, I just knew he was being good and faithful. I mean, what kind of wife don't check her man about not coming home? I never dealt with the phone calls or drama until then, so it wasn't like I was just out here being naïve, and I wasn't even that type of woman to be laid up with the next bitch's man. I didn't roll that way. I mean, let me not toot my own horn, but I'm not the ugly type, nor is my self-esteem low. I might live in the hood, but I have my own house, a job, and I take damn good care of myself. I'm light-skinned, more like kissed by the sun, blonde-crinkly dreads that hang on my shoulders, almond-shaped eyes, with a round ass, juicy lips, full breasts, and thighs. I mean come the fuck on. I'm a damn knockout!

I'd called Link's ass at least seventeen times since I'd been here, and not once did he call, text, and he damn sure didn't show up. I would think someone who was carrying your baby would be important, but I guess not. I should've seen this coming though. What the hell was I doing with a corporate man anyway? I wasn't smart enough to be with Link's ass, especially not in public. Whenever he would take me to nice places, restaurants included, I always felt out of place and almost stupid around him, even though he never said anything to me to make me feel that way. It was just the way other people looked at me or talked to me that made me feel like I was less than. I loved him, and I'd given him two years of my life, two years that I could've possibly been doing something else, but I wasn't because I was "so in love" that I waited around in a relationship that I wish I would've seen wasn't going anywhere. I did get some pretty good shit out of the relationship. He paid my bills for the most part, and don't think because a bitch lives in the projects she ain't got no bills because I do. I got a cell phone bill, nails, feet, hair, lights, water, car note, all that, and yes, ladies, beauty is a bill. Now, don't get me wrong, I paid my way too, but that doesn't mean that Link wasn't a good help. Let's also be real about one more thing, Link and Luna? That shit was cute as fuck, another reason I was blinded. I believed we were destined to be and were just taking it at a normal rate in which people date. He'd been to my house, and I'd even been to his. Where the hell was his wife when I was spending the night? Granted, he did stay at my place more often than I stayed at his, but I just thought that was him wanting to be up in my shit, but again, I'm a fucking idiot. What man wants to lay up in the projects when he practically lives in a castle?

The doctor took a needle out of her pocket and inserted it into the IV I had connected to my arm, and before the drugs started to take effect, I wanted to smack myself for being so stupid. What was I thinking, and why didn't I see the signs? Now they were just all too clear, and all of this shit could've been avoided. The doctor pretty much told me my cervix gave up on me and was bruised and damaged too bad from the three abortions I had in the past, and it couldn't support a baby. These are the things the doctor doesn't tell you when they say you have the choice to decide what to do. Yeah, pro-choice sounds great, but what the medical system should do is better educate you on what pro-choice means. Yeah, you've got the choice to decide to abort your baby, but you don't have the right to know what it can do to your baby later on down the line? That shit was crazy.

The medicine started to take a hold of me, but before it completely knocked me out, I took my phone off of the table beside me and scrolled to Link's name and sent him a hateful ass text message. He needed to know what was going on. He could lie and say he didn't get the voicemails, but he couldn't deny a text message.

To Link: You a selfish, no-good ass, dusty ass nigga. I loved you, and you took advantage of that. You got me

pregnant, and no, I don't want to be together, but I did want you to take care of your baby, speaking of which, is no longer here you asshole! I'm not gon' cry one more fucking tear over you or this situation, but I figure I'd at least let you know what was going on. I hate you, I hate you, I hate you!

I don't care about being no grown ass woman; that nigga had taken me to a place of no return, a place I never thought I could reach honestly. I was about to put my phone down when I realized I had several messages from a few different people, one of them being from the housing authority. That was weird because they hardly ever sent out text messages. They were quick to email and leave a thousand voicemails, and those damn papers on the door that I normally threw away, but since I wasn't home, I'm sure I missed the thousands of trees being killed and left on my door.

"Hello, Luna, this is Ms. Penelope in the housing office. The last two checks we've received for your rent have bounced. This is your final warning. If you don't come up with six-hundred dollars in the next three days, you'll be evicted. Also, there is a bouncing fee of forty-dollars for each check, so six-hundred and eighty dollars to be exact. When you get a chance, give me a call so we'll know how you'd like to take care of this issue."

I didn't even have the strength to call or do anything else. I was finally about to fall asleep and pray that for just a moment, all of my problems would be blasted to the past or the fuck away from me.

"Luna, Luna, if you'll sign here, you'll be able to get on out of here. Now, here are a few prescriptions. This one is to prevent infection, this one is to help with the pain, and this one is to help you sleep soundly. Also, we have written you an excuse letter as you requested. Now, if you'll just sign right here, you'll be free to go."

It felt as though I had only been asleep for a few minutes, but I'd gotten three hours of sleep. I was still in pain on the inside and all over my body. I requested the excuse note because I knew my job wasn't going to believe me if I didn't show up without one. My boss, Black, was the type of man that just assumed everything you said was a lie, but I honestly believe it was because he wasn't my type, and I wouldn't give him any play. Besides that, I was the only female that worked in the entire bar, and his family was HUGE, which meant I wound up serving a lot of them, and they were rude and acted like they ruled the world.

I hated my job; Bar Scovel was an eyesore on Bardstown Road. It had so much potential because we all know location is everything, but the location doesn't always mean a good job. I didn't even have benefits, and my tips, I had to split with Black, so I was hardly bringing home any money. Why don't I quit, you might ask? Well, if you thought this story was sad, it's about to get a hell of a lot worse.

I grew up in a house with a mother who's emotionally void where she feels nothing, no love, no happiness, and the only emotion she had was anger and sadness. That was her my entire life. She was messed up from the time she had me. She fell in love with a bad boy, my father, who she later on married, but what she didn't account for was the fact that all bad boys have their day. After a robbery gone wrong that he thought he'd staged perfectly, he was murdered. My mother was pregnant with me when it happened, so I never got the chance to meet my father, and because of that, she's always been a mess. Then when I thought she was finally getting it together emotionally with a little counseling, and a lot of me distancing myself, her health began deteriorating. I believe her stress levels were the first problem, which led to high blood pressure, which in turn took her appetite, and eventually, she became malnourished, and because of that, while I was in high school, I started missing school to take care of her.

I did the best I could, truly, but I was a child, and because of that, I didn't graduate, so without a diploma or a GED, the only place I could get a job was this ran down ass bar, Bar Scovel. I can't lie, even though I hate working for Black, this is the only job I'll be able to get, and it isn't always bad, but most of the time, it is, and it was only about to get a lot worse.

After I signed my name, it was time for me to go back home, if I even still had one. When I saw that text pop up on my phone about being evicted, I wanted to kill Link, literally murder his ass. Not only had he ripped my heart out of my chest, but now he was playing with my living situation. Why did I trust him to be a good man? Why did I believe he would take care of me? I had no one to blame but my damn self at this point, and I'd have to work extra hard if I was going to somehow come up with some money in time.

The nurse came into my room with a wheelchair, forcing me to get in because I wasn't allowed to leave walking out alone. I already had to call a Lyft with the last of my money, literally. This shit wasn't going to get any easier.

When the car stopped in front of my home, I realized the medicine started wearing off. I could feel the pain between my legs starting up again, and I hadn't even dropped off my prescription yet. I wasn't supposed to be driving, but I wasn't going to have a choice unless I wanted to become infected or remain in pain.

The housing office looked all gloom and doom as it normally did. I was embarrassed to even go inside because I didn't know how I was going to come up with that kind of money in such a short amount of time. I couldn't go back to work right away; I was allowed a few days off, per the doctor's orders, but I had a good feeling they weren't going to be trying to hear that, so I chose to not even go in there, not just yet. I was going to have to work myself up to do it.

Next, I needed to go and talk to Black. I was supposed to be in the bed resting, but rest is for people who can do whatever they want, and I certainly do not have that damn luxury. I didn't want to go down to Bar Scovel; I hated it. Night was about to fall, and things could get kind of crazy around here when it did. We were closed during the day, and I had never come in during the daytime, even though Black lived right above the bar, but that nigga was crazy. He acted like the rules he set were the truth, like there was no other way. I wasn't even allowed to go there during the day, and the way he told me when he said not to come around sent chills through my body, and I knew not to try him. On top of that, he's my boss, and I can't afford to lose this job, especially not now.

Before the evening fell, I figured I'd drop off my prescriptions, so that way when I was on my way from leaving the bar, I'd be able to pick them back up, go home, rest, and try to figure out what I was going to do, since it wasn't looking too good for me.

I had my keys in my hand, but I didn't want to open the car door to drive, but I also didn't have any more money to be taking a Lyft or a taxi. I hated my life so bad right now. I felt like a toddler who just wanted to rest and couldn't; I was so afraid of getting an infection in between my legs, lawd, I had no choice but to get over myself and get in the car.

With the keys in the ignition, I turned the radio on to distract me. I figured if I got in a good rhythm, I'd find the energy to drive myself to drop off the prescriptions, but then I thought about the hospital. They should start a service to transport you from the hospital to handle your prescriptions and shit if you aren't supposed to be driving. That made absolutely no sense. I guess once you were off their property they didn't give a damn about you. I road slowly down the street, nodding my head to Jay-Z's latest hit

"Top Off" onto Bardstown Road where the Walgreens and the bar were. I could kill two birds with one stone. As I pulled up in the drive-thru to drop off my prescription, as I was driving in, I could see the bar behind me in my rearview mirror. I must have been losing my mind because I could have sworn I saw a huge ass bird or something swoop down, but when I turned around, I didn't see anything. It left an eerie feeling inside of me, especially since the sun was now gone. Bardstown Road was one of the livest streets in Louisville, and because of that, it catered to all kinds of people. I honestly felt sometimes like there was something freaky going on over there, especially with Black's bar. There were times I wondered if they were vampires or something was wrong with them, maybe crackheads. Whenever he got upset, every now and then, I could swear his eyes turned red, but that could also be my mind. I was almost always drunk at work; that was the only way I could cope. With some of the shit I saw in there or thought I saw in there, the intoxication was more than needed.

I shrugged it off as my mind playing tricks on me and just kept going through the line. I needed to get my meds, and soon enough, I'd be in there with Black's crazy ass anyway.

☙❧

AFTER DROPPING OFF MY PRESCRIPTION, I HEADED OVER TO the bar where people were already filing in. It didn't matter to me though because I'd be off work tonight, and there would be no drinking and no serving, listening to men gripe all

night, and no disgusting customers. I hardly ever had any
female customers or saw women come into the bar anyway. It
wasn't a proper place for a woman, especially not me. I got
into fights all the time and was always in trouble with Black,
but he kept me around, and I knew why. See, Black had a
little crush on me. Everyone knew about it, including me, and
I chose to ignore him. There was nothing he could do for me
that I couldn't do for myself. Yeah, he made money, but it
wasn't that corporate type of money or that let me act right
kind of money, and he honestly scared me. There was something about him that always rubbed me wrong from the
moment I got the job at the bar, but I was too afraid to say
anything because I didn't want to lose my job. Even with
Link's help, I never wanted to be out of a job, and I refused
to lose it just because I had a slime bag boss. I could adapt
and handle any situation, and I'd made it clear that there was
no me and him nor would there ever be, and that wasn't going
to change.

I parked my car in the back of the bar and went in
through the employee entryway. Everyone else who worked at
the bar were men, and I always felt like they got special treat-
ment over me. If they wanted to call out, they could, and I'd
HAVE to come in and cover their shift, but if I dared try to
call out, it was going to be an issue, and I already knew when
I went into the bar, it was going to be some shit. I just hoped
it wasn't going to be a problem or an issue. My fingers were
crossed tighter than a nun's pussy.

I opened the door and walked in to see Black standing in
the hall smoking a cigarette with his shirt off and only his
sweatpants that were snugly tied around his waist hugging
him. If Black weren't such a dick, I'd find him attractive. He
was handsome, tatted up with some tribal tattoos that never
seemed quite finished because he had spaces that were still
open, and a curly fro that was always just fucking perfect. His

smile was always devilish like he was plotting on everyone around him. I knew I couldn't trust him, but I needed something from him, and I had to see if

he was going to act right and give it to me. I could only hope he would...

3

STONE

"NOOOOOO!" the king yelled from his place on the roof of what looked to be a warehouse.

My stone-like figure slowly began shimmering away. The thing is, when we turn back, the stone never goes away, it just goes back into us the same way it covers us. It's more like another layer of skin. It hurts, but not in the way you probably think.

I looked over to Pandora, who had her knees in her chest with her chin resting on them, crying silently. The sun had gone down, and the moon would soon be peaking out, but I wondered if the queen's remains were still there. It was a long shot, but there was only one way to find out.

"Pandora, take the king back to the realm. I'll follow shortly behind you."

"And where are you going, Stone? Don't you think you need to come with us now? This is not a safe place, especially since now I'm not stepping down from the kingdom. We need to get home to prepare for the mourning of others and a funeral."

I rubbed my hands over my face because I didn't want to say anything and get his hopes up, but I needed to say something.

"My king, no disrespect, but she was your wife first, and then your queen, so you need to mourn separately from your people. I'm going back over to the spot where...where it happened to see if we can find her remains. We will send her to the afterlife in style."

Kairo's face contorted, and Pandora rose from where she was and came over to the king.

"He's right, my king. Let me lead you home where we can make you more comfortable."

I bowed my head at Pandora. I could tell she didn't feel the same way I was feeling, because I could tell how she felt. She was broken, but I was wrecked because even in the face of conflict, I still had a duty and things to do. Part of that would be getting the queen's remains, if possible, and taking them back to the realm.

I jumped down from the building, landing right in front of Bar Scovel, and for a second, I saw the sexiest human I'd ever seen. I could only see a small glimpse of her as she was in a car, but she had dreads, that natural beauty. I had never seen a human that looked like her, but she was...she was one of a kind. I didn't have time to be looking at this woman. Now wasn't the time, and it wasn't like I could be involved with a human anyway.

I escorted them both across the street together where they could open the portal in the other side of the alley, and right there piled up to the side of the road, Queen Zaya was. Strangely enough, she was the most beautiful gargoyle I had ever seen at that point. Her stone-self wasn't like any other I'd ever seen. She wasn't making a face of pain or confusion. Her face didn't seem like that of a rushed one...she looked peaceful. I wondered if she felt any pain in her last moments. Did she know what was about to happen? How could she choose to help me, when we just had a whole conversation about sacrificing for the kingdom? The kingdom would be fine without me, but without her, there was no doubt that it would surely fall.

Kairo saw her broken body, and it was like the realization finally hit him. His wife, lover, and best friend was never coming back. His queen was gone, and he would solely have to rule on his own, without his reason for breathing. I was madder at myself than anything because I should've stopped her. I should've been the one to make sure she was in the realm safely. It should have been me to get smashed into pieces, not her.

The way they disregarded her body to the side of the road had me ready to kill every human on the road, but I couldn't do that; that wouldn't be right, not at all. It didn't stop me from thinking about it or thinking about how in reality, this was Black's fault, and no matter what I had to do or how I had to, I would make him pay for the loss we were now experiencing.

Pandora had the king by the arm, bracing herself for the impact of breaking through the barrier. She looked around to make sure no one was looking, and then with the Kairo, she disappeared into the wall, where I was thankful the two of them had at least made it safely.

I gathered the shattered pieces in my arms, determined not to drop any of them, and headed to the end of the alley to enter the realm once again. Before I stepped through, it was as if something was drawing me to the bar, but I couldn't go toward it. There was so much hurt inside, something was calling out to me, trying to get my attention, but I needed to be there for my family and the kingdom that made me who I was. At the end of the day, I was loyal to a fault, and no matter what happened, queen or no queen, I had a duty and a love for my people and the kingdom so strong. No matter what, I would be there to not only admit my fault for not being the one to be taken but face whatever consequences came behind that.

❧ 4 ❧

LUNA

"Hey, Black, can I talk to you for a second?" I asked Black as I approached him with the papers dead in my hands ready to hand to them.

He looked at me, and I could have sworn I saw his eyes light up, but not in a good way. More so with a hellish fire in them.

"Talk to me? Hopefully, it ain't to ask for your job back, 'cuz that's a no-go, Lu." "My job? I lost my job? I text you and told you I was in the hospital. How could I have lost my job? You didn't even fire me."

"Shit, you ain't tell me what you were there for either, Luna, so I thought you were lying." "Lying?" I almost broke my neck turning my head to the side to bend my body up in confusion. "Here, you tell me if I'm lying or not," I said, handing him the papers to go over.

As he flipped through them, I could tell when he saw at the top where it said I lost my baby, that he was confused. I hadn't told anyone I was pregnant, at least anybody outside of Link. I hadn't even told my mother. Not because I didn't want to, but because I heard it was bad luck to be talking about that stuff till you got to at least five months, so I'd kept it to myself.

"Damn, Luna, I'm sorry. Why didn't you tell me you were pregnant? I'm, shit, I'm sorry you lost your baby and shit. You can have your job back, but you ain't dressed for work." "Excuse me?" I asked with an attitude. I know this nigga didn't just say I wasn't dressed for work.

"You ain't dressed for work. Ok, you lost your baby, but you here now, so what else would you be here for than to work?"

"I came to drop off these papers so you could see the doctor said I need to rest for the next few days, to take it easy so that you would understand why I wouldn't be coming in." Black tucked the papers in between his armpits and got closer to me. I felt the hairs on my arm stand up because I wasn't sure what he would do.

"Luna, you come to work tonight, work the register. You ain't gotta be on your feet. Some of the other guys are here or should be, so they can serve, but they can't run the register like you can. Hell, not even I can, so I'ma need you. I'll see you at eleven, right?"

I couldn't believe this shit. I wanted to cry and yell and let this bastard know that I wouldn't be coming in, but how could I? I was on the verge of eviction, and I needed the money, really bad. If I was going to be coming into work, he was going to have to give me something in return.

"Fine, you want me to work tonight, I need a favor. Can I get an advance on my check? You know I thought Link's ass was paying my rent, turns out his checks bounced. I don't know what that was about, because that first check he sent was before I even found out about him cheating, so I don't know what else to do. If you could give me an advance, I'll work extra hard and stay extra late if need be."

Black stroked his goatee as he thought about it, at least

what I thought he was thinking about. He raised his hand, and I jumped back, afraid of what might happen. He grabbed a handful of my dreads and pushed them behind my shoulder.

"Luna, if you needed money, all you had to do was ask. You don't have to work any harder than you're already working...you know what I want from you," he said as he licked his lips. Oh hell no, there was no way he was trying to proposition me.

"Are you serious right now, Black? I need the money, but not that damn bad to where I would sleep with you." I told him "Sleep with me? You think I want you to sleep with me? Nah, baby, I want a little head, that's all. You ain't never had no dick like this, I can promise you that."

"Yuck! Do not make me fucking gag! I wouldn't put your dick in my mouth if it was the fucking cure to cancer. I'll see you when it's time for my shift to start."

I snatched the hospital discharge papers back out of his armpit and stormed off back to my car. I could feel his eyes on me the entire way. Who the fuck did he think he was? Like nigga, you can't get pussy of your own, you gotta "pay" for it? And I'm not even a prostitute. I'm telling you, niggas always think because a bitch is from the hood that she's about that hoe life, and I just wasn't raised like that, nor would I ever be like that. I was able to get a project because I had sick mother who I was taking care of at one point, till she got to the point that she didn't want to stay with me anymore and wanted to live in her own house, but the housing authority didn't need to know that. That shit wasn't any of their business, and as far as I knew, they didn't know either, or they would've been evicted my little ass.

In my car, I let out a few tears, but nothing too much. I couldn't let myself get that upset over something I knew I wasn't going to stop taking, and after I paid off this rent situation and got caught up, I was going to start paying for the

GED class so I could take the test. There had to be something better out there for me than this life of working in a trashy bar and living in a project. Truth be told, I always thought I'd be a stylist of some sort. Picking out celebrity's clothes and shit. I was always dressed to the max, but I did shop on a budget, which to me is what made me so good at dressing myself. I didn't spend a fortune to look cute; I had a strict budget and stuck to it.

The clock on my car radio let me know my prescription was probably ready since the lady said it would only take about forty minutes. I headed back to the pharmacy to pick up my medicine, and then I went home to take the pain meds, lay down, and to prepare for my night at work.

5

STONE

"I'll be by your side, my king, no matter what."

"Stone, I don't know how I will do this. What am I to say to those who depend on us? What of the Scovel clan? I will have to go back on my word, and a king never goes back on his word."

"A king can do whatever he sees fit, but now is not the time to worry about any of that. I told you, you need to take time to mourn your loss, you aren't ready to speak just yet. You need to wait."

"I can't wait. Don't you see? The longer I hide this from the people, the worse it will become. There is something I haven't told you, and I prayed I would never have to, but now that the time is upon us, I...I don't know what to say," Kairo said as he stumbled backwards, leaning up against the wall. I reached my hand out for him to take.

"Tell me what? What don't I know?" Pandora stormed through the door, pushing it wide open. "My king, something is wrong, several of the others have fallen...they appear to be sleeping, but with no heartbeat."

"No, no, not so soon!"

"Not so soon, what? Tell me, what is it?" I asked, confused as to what she meant and what the king said.

"Pandora, come here, my child."

Pandora came closer, and I pulled up a chair for Kairo to sit in.

"When one of us passes on, the entire line goes with us. Everyone from the queen's family, cousins, aunts, and what not will also perish. There are many others here, but it has already begun."

"How can we stop it? Who will we lose? How many?" I asked, panicking.

"Thousands, and not just the ones who are here, the ones in the human world who have the queen's descendants blood will also perish. It is the way it has always been. No one and nothing was truly meant to last forever."

"And what does that mean for me? I come from the both of you, you and her, surely I'll die as well."

"That is a question that only Jonas can answer, but my greatest guess would be that you need to mate, so that you and Pandora may rule, and then, you won't have to worry about passing away, at least not for a very, very long time. The kings and queens, during the ceremony of union, undergo a special spell that can make you almost immortal, but not really, as nothing lives forever. You, Stone, are the closest thing we have to an immortal, and the closest thing we have to a son. The throne should have rightfully been yours, but you've made it more than clear that was not something you wanted."

I had to think about everything he was saying right now. I didn't want to be a king; I had seen the sacrifices and everything else it took, and I couldn't say it was something I was willing to do. I'd been alive for so long, I had gotten accustomed to being a protector; I couldn't imagine being anything else. A king wasn't a protector—essentially, being a king was being a dictator. Telling others what to do and then them doing it, and I didn't want that. I liked being able to carry out the will of the kingdom, and becoming king just wasn't it. I didn't want to die either. I needed to have this confirmed before I just jumped the gun though.

When I looked over at Pandora, she had a huge grin on her face, and I knew what she was thinking because I could feel it. She was going to take this shit and run with it. Pandora knew I would do anything for the success of the kingdom, even if it meant truly mating with her ass, but at this point, it was something I was unsure of. Before, it seemed like I had a choice in the matter, but now, I wasn't feeling that choice; it seemed more like something I had to do, even though I didn't want it, and then Black popped into my head.

"If I become king, what does that mean for Black and the Scovel clan, what does that mean for you?

What will happen to you?" The king put his head down and shook his head. I knew this couldn't be good. "If you become king, I will move on to the afterlife in peace. I won't have to die a violent death, and you'll have to deal with Black yourself."

"Myself? Not that I care, but that's kind of harsh. Nobody told you to make an agreement like this in the first place. Where are the fucking advisors when you need them? Even more so, this will bring about more war. What will happen to your bloodline, the direct descendants of your family?"

"They too shall perish."

"This makes no fucking sense! Somebody get Jonas. Pandora, go find him now!" I roared, flashing my stone-gray eyes at her. I could see the conflict inside of her. She wanted to argue with me, to make me commit to something I wasn't trying to do, but she knew I was too strong for that. Pandora turned around to get him, but she never closed the door, so he was able to walk straight in.

"You called for me, my king?"

"No, I called for you! What the fuck is going on? Is there a way around this? Will I have to mate with Pandora to stay alive, to keep the kingdom from being usurped, even though they made an agreement?"

"The agreement was never made final. We didn't sign anything. Therefore, it's our words against theirs."

"Your word is your bond, Kairo. Isn't that what you taught me? You have nothing if you can't keep your word."

"Yes, and that, my son, was the wrong thing to teach you. When it comes to love, it will always trump everything else. I would do anything for Zaya, and I did, and now that she's gone, I can't live this life, in this kingdom, without her by my side, without her as my queen. I would have gladly stepped down with her and lived a semi-regular gargoyle life, but without her, it's pointless, and I won't see my kingdom go to hell because of it."

Kairo pulled his royal robes to the side and went over to the bookshelf, his sacred bookshelf. Of all the places in the kingdom, this was the only place that was forbidden to be touched. His collection was legendary; not even Jonas had access to it. Everyone respected the king entirely too much to disobey him, even me. When he returned, he had two books in his hand and passed them to Jonas.

"I'm not sure if these will help, but I came across them a hundred years or so ago when I was in the human world. Perhaps there's a spell in here that can help with Stone. Will he die if I die?"

Jonas had a worried look on his face, and I could tell he didn't even know the answer, which only frustrated me more.

"My king, I do not know the answer in which you seek. I hope he will not. I made him as close to immortal as I possibly could, but there is no telling, truly. Even more so, if you go...I come from your line of ancestry, I too will die."

I turned to look at Jonas. This was some more shit I didn't know. All the time I'd spent learning about our people and how to defend them, I never knew anything about our real ancestry or the things that made us who we were, not the important shit anyway.

"So what do we do at this point, Jonas? How do we fix this?" I asked, pacing the floor back and forth.

Jonas rubbed his chin in deep thought, looking at all of us.

"I say, you truly mate with Pandora, ceremony and all. We celebrate the queen's passing into the afterlife before all of that, of course, and we can send the king into hiding for some time. Perhaps one of our allied clans will take him in."

"Take me in? I'm not a refugee, and I don't want to be taken in. I want to pass on to the afterlife so I can be with my wife, my true love. This life is not worth living without her, I can assure you of that."

I wished I could feel that. I wanted so badly to know what that feeling was like, to have someone who was so much of you that you felt like you couldn't breathe without them, and Pandora was not it for me. "What say you, Stone? Will, you mate with Pandora and become one, so that the kingdom may continue to flourish? The king has made it clear that he doesn't want to be amongst the living any longer. We can put him to sleep and send him on peacefully so that he can run into Zaya's arms once more."

Pandora looked at me, and her eyes filled with tears. I hated to do this to her, and how could I? I didn't want to be the gargoyle to break her heart, because forever was a long time to carry that type of burden, but what else was I going to do? I needed to focus my energies elsewhere, or I was going to lose it.

"First things first, I need to handle Black before I make

any decisions. I need to make sure this won't initiate some full-on out war, because it could be dangerous. I'll go speak with him by myself, and I'll see what I can do about the agreement you made, and see how dishonoring it will turn out, even though I have a pretty good idea. Jonas, in the meantime, look in those books and see if you can find anything that will save me if necessary."

I turned to walk out of the king's room when I felt a hand reach out to me. "And what should I do, Stone?" "Pandora, do what you do best. Stay here and look after our people."

I wasn't completely heartless; I just didn't want to mate with her. She would be the perfect match for someone who had no personality, just not me. I had way too much life inside of me to be with someone so dull who only cared about sex and the kingdom.

6

LUNA

"*That smile on your face makes it easy to trust you...*" Partynextdoor's *Break From Toronto* played from my phone as my alarm, as it always did. I was surprised I was even able to wake up. Talk about being tired and in pain, but Black promised I could work on the register tonight and not have to serve anyone. He had me fucked up anyway if he thought I was going to. My lower body was in more pain than it had ever been, and I could barely stand. I was really about to go to work because I needed the paycheck, but if Black wanted me to continue working there, he was going to have to show me some cash, so I could pay my rent off. If not, I was going to be put out. Sure, I would be able to stay for another thirty days, and I'd probably have to go to court, but the court fees wouldn't even be worth all of that.

Grabbing my phone, I pulled the covers off of my face and began sending a message to Black, but before I could, he'd already sent me one.

Black: I'm not going to be in the bar tonight, just wanted to let you know. But don't worry, I got the

serving part taken care of for you. Just run the register like I asked, and you're good. 😉

I smirked at that, and not in a good way. His winky face emoji made me want to throw up because a part of him repulsed me, and I couldn't figure out what it was. I had met plenty of men like him before, but he was like a snake, something about him just wasn't right. It was fine that he was going to leave me in there with the guys tonight. It wasn't like that was any different than any other night, so it wasn't a big deal. I still needed that money, and this was as good a time as any to mention it again. This time, I had to let him know I would quit and walk away, and I needed to sound convincing if I was going to make him give it to me.

Me: Ok, that's cool and all, but check it out, if you want me to keep working for you, I need something. I already asked you earlier, and you almost made me quit, for real. I didn't want to say this earlier because I was so mad, but if you can't give me an advance, I'm going to go work at Wild Eggs where I'll make money for serving. I was already offered the job, so the ball is in your court. I know six-hundred, and eighty dollars is a lot of money, so don't advance me for that much, but I will need at least three-hundred and forty dollars to at least help. I figure half is better than none, so let me know. 😊

I put my phone down and slid out of bed, heading to my bathroom for a shower. As soon as I cut the water on and the steam began to fill the room, I heard my phone ding. I knew it was Black texting me back, but I wasn't about to let him ruin my shower by reading that text that I'm sure was going to piss me off, so I stepped out of my clothes and got into the shower, letting the water cascade down my body.

As the water fell over my body, all I could think about was Link and how I missed his touch and how he used to fuck me. Damn, I missed him so much. It was more than just the sex

47

too. He made my project feel like a mansion the way he fixed it up for me, and that was another reason I didn't want to leave this muthafucka. It was nice as hell, and I had the nicest project around, or shit, to have ever been made, okkuurrt?

On top of that, I never felt lonely with Link. He was smart, funny, sweet, and he had such an amazing life. We were able to go to all types of places, and he was just cool to be around. I could tell him anything, and he was always there for me, but now, I had no one. I couldn't tell my mother, I didn't want to bother her with my problems. I didn't want to hurt her heart any more than it already was. She was mad at me for not finishing high school, even though I quit to take care of her. She was mad that I stayed in this project even after she moved out, but I couldn't afford another place, not yet. She was pissed that I never went to college. It was too much; every time I talked to her I just felt guilty as fuck, and I couldn't handle that right now, especially since losing the baby. Every now and then I would send her a text to let her know I was thinking of her or to ask if she needed anything. Sometimes I would drop stuff off to her or come to take care of her, but for the most part, she would push me out of the house or pretend like she was doing just fine, but I knew her and knew when something wasn't right. I let it slide, but don't get that twisted with me not giving a fuck. We gotta let our parents be who they gon' be, just like they gotta let us be who we gon' be regardless.

After I soaped up and washed my body, I stepped out of the shower and rubbed my hands across the fogged up mirror to look at myself. Though I was beautiful on the outside, I couldn't help but think about how ugly I must have been on the inside to not be able to get ahead in life. I felt like I must have done something in the past that brought about all this unwanted bad karma. What did I do to piss God off so bad that he took the best man or thing that ever happened to me away? I know I've pretty much only made it seem like he was a financial blessing to me, and even though that's true, that's not just it. He was my world. He was everything to me. I lost myself in him, so much so, that now...I don't know. I don't even know how to act around people at this point. I truly just wanted to be around him, but I was too strong to let a nigga completely take me out. Especially a nigga with a million kids that he NEVER mentioned, not one time. Any nigga who would run away from his responsibilities is a coward ass nigga anyway if we're being completely honest.

I pulled my dreads up into a high bun, leaving three down in the front for a little bang action and one down in the back just because that shit is cute! I was too tired to be putting on a full face of makeup, not tonight baby, not tonight, so I came out of my bathroom and opened my drawer to slip on my granny panties. Tonight, I wasn't trying to be cute. From the waist down I needed to be comfortable, and if I didn't have to wear a bra, I wouldn't have! But my breasts were too big to be doing all that, and it just enticed people too much with your nipples all hard and shit, so I put on my black bra. Then pulled open my bottom drawer to pull out my blue jean Bermuda shorts and threw on my all-white flowy tank top. It kind of blew in the wind and made me feel angelic and shit, so that was the fit for the night with my classic all-white Converses. There was no need to be being extra cute. I wasn't going to be making any tips tonight, just standing behind the register ringing up shit, so nope, I had to keep it moving.

My phone dinged again, and I wondered if it was a reminder text or if Black had text me again, so I picked my phone up, and it was three texts. Ii must have missed one while in the shower.

Black: Girl, shut the fuck up. If you were going to another place, you would've been gone. I'm not givin' you no damn three hundred dollars, you must be crazy.

49

Black: So you not gon' respond? You still goin' to work tonight though, right?

Black: Luna, my bad, baby, yeah, I'm 'bout to slide by your mailbox now and put the money in it. Have a good night at work.

Please go in there and take care of the place. Shit wouldn't be right without you there.

I smiled and flopped on the bed. That shower might have just been what saved my life! I didn't know how the housing authority would react to only having half, but half was better than nothing, and I had something to bargain with now. If nothing else, shit, I could save that damn money in case of a rainy day that I would surely have if they didn't accept the half payment.

I didn't want to take any more medicine before work, but I wasn't sure how I'd make it through the night without it. I was starting to feel it all over my body again, and I didn't want to be at work passing out with cramps that weren't cramps—they were more like death stabs, and that shit was killing me. I just prayed they didn't have a serious effect on me and that Black kept his promise.

My keys were by the door, and so was my purse, so

I grabbed my things and headed out the door and to the mailbox. Before I flipped the flap open, I took a deep breath. Surely, he wasn't fucking with me, but this is Black we're talking about. I popped the little flappy door open and reached my hand inside feeling around the walls, and at first, I didn't feel anything. Just when I was about to close it, there was something at the bottom it seemed that kept scratching my hand, so I got on my tippy toes and stuck my hand all the way in and pulled out an envelope.

Ripping the envelope open, I pulled out the money and started counting it. He'd put four-hundred dollars in. I'd never been so happy in my life! I was so hype, I jumped up and down holding the money close to my heart like it was a jewel or something.

"THANK YOU LAWD!" I shouted rather loudly and looked around to make sure nobody could see me and jumped in my car to head to work.

❧ 7 ❧

TWO HOURS LATER...

STONE

I sat at a table in the corner for hours waiting for Black to show up, trying to stay out of the way. I could tell by the way everyone was interacting nobody knew about the queen's death, and that was a good thing. I didn't want them to know just yet, and I needed to discuss it with Black first. If he was in his right mind, he'd know to control his people. I was about to give up and call it a night, go get in my bed and start fresh tomorrow with everything that needed to be done, but then I felt a presence around me that was unfamiliar. There was something in the air that I'd never smelled before. Whatever it was...if I could compare it to peace, then I would. Something about it relaxed me and made me feel... like I was at home, so I let the feeling lead me and take me to the bar, and there she was, the girl I'd seen in the car for just a moment. The closer I got to her, I could smell and feel the pain in her body. I wondered if she was sick...this was one of the weirdest feelings I'd ever had. I'd only ever had this connection with Pandora, and I didn't want it with her, but this...this human, she had me confused, and I liked it. She was something like a challenge.

When I approached the bar, she was sitting at the register, taking someone's order. I had to give it to Black, he had some good items, or what seemed like they were. I loved to eat, and he had good appetizers like cheese sticks, breadsticks, personal pizzas, and chicken tenders—all food that went well with liquor. Not that I was much of a drinker, but with the way I was feeling, shit, I could use a drink; but I had business to tend to, so drinking wasn't going to happen tonight.

"Excuse me, sweetheart, can you tell me where Black is?" I asked, tapping on the bar lightly. "Uhm, who's asking?" She looked into my face, and when our eyes locked, it was like nothing I'd ever experienced in my life. My heart felt like it would turn to stone right there. She was examining me, and I was doing the same to her, but not her physical. I could hear her heart beating, something I probably shouldn't have been able to, but I could. Maybe I was imagining the shit, but she had this gargoyle's mind gone.

"Uhm, I'm Stone. I needed to discuss some business with him."

"He's not here. He said he wasn't going to be coming in. Is there a message or a phone number I can give him for you?" She smiled, and my dick stiffened in my pants. I had to calm down. I had never been this easily aroused, but this was the first person I'd ever truly ever been attracted to. Pandora was cute, but she was easy, something I could have because in a way she belonged to me, but not this beautiful woman.

"Did you hear me, Stone, you said? Interesting name."

I hadn't even realized she asked me anything at all.

"My bad. There's no number to leave. I can just come back tomorrow if that's ok."

"Fine by me. I'm sure he'll be back in."

I nodded my head. My feet wanted to move, but I couldn't get my body to go with it. I needed to get back to the realm if I wasn't going to be discussing the situation with Black, but this woman was just gorgeous.

"Well, let me ask you a question. Since I gave you my name, what's yours?"

She smirked and leaned over from the barstool she was sitting on and yelled loudly, "Luna!"

"Like the moon?"

"Exactly! My mother used to tell me this story about how the moon and sun fell in love when they were still one. One day, they separated because the world needed them both, but in order to be what the world needed, they had to live separately and only be together during an eclipse. She compared that to her relationship with my father. They were madly in love, but they lived in two different worlds, figuratively speaking. She was the moon, and he was the sun, so, she named me Luna."

Luna and Stone? To me, our names were poetic. Like the moonlight shines on rocks type of shit. I had to get away from this captivating woman before I got myself into trouble, but I couldn't leave.

"That's an amazing story. Your parents must have loved you very much."

"I can't say, at least not for my father. He was dead before I was even born, and my mother, well, that just tore her up. So for a while, because of how distant she was, I thought she didn't love me, but now

I know better."

"I'm sure your father loved you. How could he not? Who do you look the most like?" I had to know if she had a mother as beautiful as she was; that would be a dangerous combination.

"I look just like my father, another reason my mother was emotionally withdrawn from years. She was denied the actual right of seeing my father every day but had to look at me, a poor clone of her true

Love...I'm sorry, I don't know why I'm just telling you all of this."

"It's ok. I've been told I have that kind of face that makes you want to bear your soul to it." I lied. Nobody had ever said anything like that to me, not once.

"Mmm...I think you're right. You're funny. Well, Mr. Stone, can I get you something to drink?"

"Nah, I'm not drinking tonight. I think that would make things worse honestly."

"Things? Things like what? You must have a lot on your mind that you need to remember to not want to drink your sorrows or whatever it is away."

"If you only knew..."

"Well, why don't you lay it on me?"

I felt the gargoyle inside me dying to growl, but I had to keep it in. I would lay something on her alright.

"You never know, I might be able to give you some advice. As a bartender, that's kind of my job. You know, on some therapeutic type shit. I'm not serving tonight, but I'd be happy to serve you."

I couldn't tell if I was making this shit up, but it seemed like she was licking her lips and teeth when she was talking to me. I couldn't pay that any attention or I'd pull her over this counter. Strangely enough, no one seemed to be bothered by my presence, which let me know they weren't about that life, or they didn't know I was in there. It was crazy to me, but I was happy for no drama. Now I could spend some time with the beautiful Luna.

"Well, I don't know where to start," I said, wondering if I should really get into the problem. I could use someone unbiased to the situation to talk to, so it couldn't hurt to get it off my chest.

"I'ma just go ahead and tell you that this is kind of a lot. I was...adopted if you will, kind of, by distant relatives, but not as distant as you would imagine, and my family is what some would call royalty. They're rich and have the status, but my... what would be called my mother I guess, passed away, and because of that, it's kind of thrown the house into disarray. My father wants me to take over the family business because now he's ready to step down, but I don't want it. I'm happy doing what I do now, and I don't want to give up my life as I know it, but I want to make them proud and honor their name and legacy."

Luna leaned across the bar and nodded her head up and down. "You need a drink, and you're getting one whether you want it or not."

She stood from the bar stool she was in and turned around to get one of the bottles down, and I couldn't help but run my eyes down her backside. She was beautiful from the front and the back. She had beautiful, toned legs, and I loved her shape.

When she turned back around, she had a shot glass and a brown bottle in her hand.

"What's that?" I asked, smelling the foul liquid in the cup.

"Bourbon, it's good for the nerves. Take it to the head."

At this point, hell, I would've taken a damn poison apple from her, she was that beautiful. I didn't wanna look like a punk, so I took the cup and threw it back, letting the liquor burn my throat, and I felt it when it landed in my stomach.

"Good, now that you've got that out the way let me pour you another one while I give you some advice. I don't mean to be harsh, but it already sounds like you know what the fuck you want, so do it! Don't try and live up to someone else's standards of what you should do or who you should be, or else you'll always be miserable. If you don't live for yourself, you'll spend the rest of your life chasing after something that you can't catch. Now, that doesn't mean don't try to appease your father, give him something that will still make him happy, but let him know that you're not going to take over the business just because he wants you to. What is it that you do anyway?"

I threw the second shot down and slammed the cup down on the bar, thinking quickly of what to say.

"Uhm, protection services."

"Oh, ok, so you're like security? Cool, so tell your dad that you want to be happy and you choose yourself. That's the only way to fix this problem, and don't think that makes you selfish, because it doesn't. Don't feel bad for choosing yourself over the stressful stigma around being in your father's shadow."

Luna reached out for my hand and stroked the top of it, and when she touched me, it seemed like something shifted around me, like there was something changing in the atmosphere.

"I think you're right, Luna. You sure you weren't a therapist in a past life?"

"Nope, just a bartender who knows a lil' sumn, sumn."

She sat back down, and we continued to talk through the rest of the night. The bar was about to close, which I figured was because the gargoyles would be turning soon, and they would need somewhere to turn without being in eyesight. They'd be more comfortable here than outside on the top of a building. Inside they'd be safe from bird shit, rain, and all types of other shit.

"Well, Stone, it's time for me to get up out of here. It's two a.m., and the bar is about to close for the night. I can honestly say it was a pleasure to meet you."

"As can I. Do you think I could walk you to your car, just to make sure you get there safely?"

She came from around the bar and smiled and reached

out for my hand. "Absolutely," she said with her hand still out. I had never held hands in an intimate way before, usually just as a battle strategy or during sex with Pandora, but that was to keep her from moving all around. I took her hand though; something about this made it seem like it would feel too good, and I needed that right now.

I grabbed her hand, and she led us to her car that was parked right out back. She hit the alarm on her car, and the red mobile's lights came on, showing the car's color a little better.

"Well, here we are, Stone. Thanks for walking with me. That was really...nice." She shrugged her shoulders like she wasn't sure.

"Nah, I was doing what any man who has been entertained by a lovely woman such as you should do. Any man who wouldn't is selfish and only cares about himself. Here, let me get your door for you."

Her face turned bloodshot red, and it was so cute. It took everything in me not to bite her little cheeks they were so swollen with heat. I opened her door for her, and she slid into the car. After I made sure she was in safely, I shut her door behind her and waited for her to start her car and pull off.

She stuck her key in the ignition and turned the key, and it made a sick sound like it was dying. Her engine coughed like it was spitting up blood. She rolled her window down with a defeated look on her face, and I gave her a soft smile.

"You wouldn't happen to know anything about cars, do you?"

I wasn't no punk ass gargoyle, but come on, we didn't have cars in the realm, and didn't need them. Shit, if something was too far away, we had wings to get us there; we were the form of transportation, so hell no I didn't know shit about no damn car.

"Unfortunately, I do not. How far do you live? I could

walk with you if it's close enough." I wanted to fly her home, but I already knew risking exposure was a no-go.

"Well...."

She seemed a bit unsure, and I wasn't sure if she didn't want me to know where she lived, or what the problem was.

"I promise if you never want to see me again afterwards, I'll never be a problem for you. I just want to make sure you make it safely."

"No, it's not that. I just...recently had a procedure done, and I'm in some pain, so I shouldn't be walking."

"Then you won't walk. I'll carry you."

She was out of her car now, shaking her head and moving her hands in a no motion, but I wouldn't let her protest. I just picked her up and slid her around to my back.

"Stoooneee!" She giggled as she said my name, and it made my dick thump against my pants.

"Hush, and just show me where to go."

She wrapped her arms around my neck and her legs around my waist and pointed in the direction we should go. I was glad her purse was one of those across the shoulder ones because I didn't know how she would've held on otherwise.

I had never done so much for a woman before, but I was liking it. Being around Luna kept me from thinking about the things I didn't want to, but soon, the night would be over, and I would have to return home to deal with my real life.

8

LUNA

The fact that this man was legitimately carrying me was fucking me up. I had NEVER met a man like this in my life. He was so big and chocolatey. He looked like a giant ass chocolate bar, and that pretty ass hair he had, and his beard. JESAWS! Lawd, give me the strength. My pussy was hurting, but I couldn't help but feel some type of way down there. I had to keep it cool.

Though I didn't live that far from the bar, I lived far enough, and for him to carry me all the way, he was dedicated. I felt bad that I couldn't give him some pussy because shit, he was working for it, but something about him said that wasn't what he was wanting, at least not right now. There was something about him that was different, and I liked it. In fact, I loved it, and talking to him, even for just a few hours made me forget about Link and how badly he hurt me. He had me looking at all men kind of sideways, but with Stone, I don't know. I thought Link was a straight up type of dude, but now I don't even know if I can trust my damn judgment for real.

When we got into my neighborhood, I started to feel

insecure, something I was familiar with, but still, I didn't want to feel like this. Stone seemed like he came from someplace nice, and I was a ghetto girl through and through. I had a nice place on the inside, but the outside looked like all the other houses, a fucking mess. I started trying to get off of his back, but he just hiked me up higher, holding more tightly onto me.

"You can let me down here, I can walk the rest of the way."

"Nah, I'ma take you the whole way. Where we goin'?"

I sighed in exasperation because I realized this probably wasn't going to lead anywhere but to an argument.

"2546, the last one on the left, right up there."

He nodded his head, and he kept walking. He didn't stop until he got onto my porch, and I was so glad to be home. I truthfully just wanted to slide in my bed and pass the fuck out, but I was also having so much fun with Stone, I wasn't ready for him to leave me just yet, but I was also too scared to ask him to come up, and I didn't want to move too fast. Link and I had just broken up, and I didn't want to seem like a fast type of girl. I just knew what I wanted, and I didn't want to be alone.

"Well, this is me...thanks for walking me home, Stone."

"Absolutely. It was my pleasure."

"I uhm....I don't know what you might have going on for the rest of the night...but...maybe you want to come upstairs and hang out some more? I know it's late, and I don't want you to feel...."

When he placed his fingers on my lips, I almost hit the ground.

"If you want me to come up, just open the door, and I'll follow behind you," he all but whispered. His voice was deep and raspy, but so sexy at the same time.

But he didn't have to tell me twice. I stuck my key in the

door so fast, you would've thought I had to pee the way I was moving. When we got into my "apartment," I clicked the lights on, and Stone stepped in, closing the door behind him.

"It smells good in here, what's that smell?"

"It smells like summertime, doesn't it? It's fresh rain by Glade."

"Mmm...I like it. You smell like it too. I could smell it when I got up on you."

I flicked my neck in his direction. He had some good ass senses to be able to smell my house on me.

"Well, if you want, we can sit down here or go upstairs. It's totally up to you."

He looked around, surveying the apartment, I guess trying to figure it out for himself.

"We can stay down here. I'm cool with that."

"Ok, great. I'm going to be right back. I'll put my things up and be right back."

I went up the stairs and went into my room to slip into my pajama pants and a t-shirt. I even took off my bra. I wasn't trying to be cute, and hell, I was tired. I didn't want to be alone, so hopefully, I could trust that he wouldn't be ogling my breasts, but I felt like even if he was, I might like it from him.

I slipped on my fuzzy house shoes and grabbed my medicine bottle and headed down the stairs. "Can I offer you something to drink? I think I have some Coke, Sprite, and Kool-Aid."

"Kool-Aid? What's that?"

I had to clutch my imaginary pearls. I know he didn't ask me what Kool-Aid was.

"Seriously, you've never had any?"

"Nah, I think I'd remember a name like that for sure."

"Well, tonight, you're about to get some. I've got the red kind, and it's the best kind there is. You want something to eat? I'm about to pop some popcorn so I can take this medicine."

"No, that's ok. I'm not hungry, but I'll take some of this Kool-Aid. You never told me what kind of procedure you had, by the way."

If someone else had of asked me that, I probably would've been defensive, but for some reason, I felt comfortable telling him, but I wanted to wait until I came out of the kitchen to do it.

"Here's your Kool-Aid, and I brought a bowl for the popcorn for if you change your mind."

I got comfortable on the couch next to him and cut the TV on, for background noise.

"I was pregnant, but I lost the baby. They had to give me a procedure, so I didn't get an infection, and to make sure they uhm...cleaned my insides out properly."

When he reached toward me, I was surprised. I expected him just to say ok, or nod his head, maybe even a sorry, but for him to pull me to him...that had completely thrown me the fuck off. Stone pulled me into his lap and held me tightly in his arms. His big, strong arms that almost squeezed the pain out of me. I was falling into a trance in his embrace when I heard him speak.

"I'm so sorry to hear that. How did the father take it?"

"Good question. I haven't seen or heard from him."

I leaned forward to grab a handful of popcorn and then grabbed the glass of red liquid.

"Here, you didn't taste your drink. Take a sip. If you don't like it, you don't have to drink it."

He took the glass from my hand and tilted his head back, and his eyes widened like they would pop out of his head.

"Ahh nah, you don't need to be drinkin' that stuff. It's gonna tear up your liver, Luna. It's super sweet. Shit!" he yelled, putting his fingers up to his neck, shaking it around, putting his tongue on the roof of his mouth, acting like he was trying to filter it through his system.

"Stop, Stone! It ain't that bad."

"Maybe not to you. Maybe it's an acquired taste kind of thing. Wooh, I can see I wasn't missing anything."

I lightly tapped his chest, and he grabbed me even tighter, bringing my face close to his. His breath against my lips felt so good, and it was strong. Not like stinky, but I could feel it, and it felt good to even have his breath close to me.

I wasn't sure if I was ready to share an intimate moment like this, so I leaned back up and grabbed my medicine bottle and opened it, pouring out two blue pills to take and took them with my sugar-aid and waited for them to take effect.

I sat in Stone's lap for an hour before I started to feel tired as hell, so I slid out of his lap and laid down on the couch and got comfortable. There was a throw blanket on the back of the couch, and Stone grabbed it and covered me with it. This man was heaven sent, but I couldn't get too excited. Getting this hype would only prove to be embarrassing later on, so I'd try to enjoy it while I could because nothing this good could happen to me.

"Goodnight, Luna, thank you for having me over.

I hope to see you around sometime."

Stone rose from the couch and headed toward the door, but I didn't want to watch him leave. Something about it was hurting my feelings.

"Stone?" I called out to him before he opened the door.

"Yes, Luna?" The way he said my name brought chills through my body.

"Will you stay with me, just until I fall asleep?

Please?"

He looked like he was conflicted, and who was I kidding?

Somebody that damn fine had to have somebody to go the fuck home to, and I was probably keeping him.

"If you don't want to, that's o—"

"Lay down, and don't worry your pretty little dread head. I'll stay till you're sound asleep. Now get comfortable and focus on sleep."

Shit, he was like my daddy, and I liked that shit. Not in an actual daddy way, but like a zaddy kind of way. Don't act like y'all don't know what I'm talking about.

Stone sat back down on the couch, and I lifted my legs up and put them on his lap, and soon after, I was asleep...but not for long.

Somehow in the middle of the night, I had flipped over on my stomach, and my head was facing the window. I couldn't be sure, but I thought I saw Stone fly out of the damn window. This medicine was going to be the death of me, and this was why I didn't want to take it in the first damn place! I knew it was tearing me up, and I'm just thankful now that my car didn't start. If I was hallucinating, I could've killed my damn self.

9

STONE

Before I left and went to the roof, which wasn't very high up, I took one last look at Luna and admired her as sleeping beauty. Though I didn't want to have pity for her, I almost couldn't help it. She seemed to be going through a lot, and for some reason, that just made me want to be around her more. I don't know if it was the fact that she lost her baby and still managed to get up, or if it was the way she laughed, her smell, her scent. I don't know, but she was doing something to me that I shouldn't have been allowing to happen.

From her window, I checked to make sure nobody was coming or looking, and I stuck my body out of the window and let my wings carry me up to the roof where I'd be sleeping until the sun went back down. Over the horizon, I could see the sky beginning to turn, and as always, it was beautiful. It was hard watching the sun come up to meet you, knowing that you'd never get to enjoy a day in the human world with the sun. Sure, the sun rose and went down in the realm too, but it was different here. This was the longest I'd ever been here before and thought I didn't want to admit it, I kind of liked it.

Finding a comfortable place on top of Luna's building, I wrapped my wrings around my body and waited for the sun to embrace me.

❧ 10 ❧

LUNA

When I finally woke up, it was two o'clock in the afternoon, and I felt like someone had run me over with a damn truck. Like, what the hell was I thinking when I decided to have company till the wee hours of the night? I didn't even have time to relax because as soon as I opened my eyes, I remembered I needed to go down to the housing authority office to see if they were going to take my little money and make something out of it, or if I needed to be taking this money to put it somewhere else like a hotel room or something. I could always stay with my mother, but I needed my freedom. I liked to be able to come and go as I pleased, and if I needed to stay at my mom's, she would be trying to control me and tell me where I could and couldn't go, and I didn't want to hear that. I'm a grown woman, I don't need a curfew, but it was a respect issue, and I didn't want to have to worry about respecting or disrespecting that lady.

Maneuvering myself off the couch was a task indeed. My legs were sore like I'd been fucking all night, but really, it was because I was sitting up at the bar last night when I should've been stretched out, elevating my feet relaxing. I was completely violating by even going into work, but I had to do it, or I felt I had to anyway. Even though Black gave me that money, there was a part of me that still felt like he was going to try me; I didn't know how or when, but I could feel it bubbling in my spirit.

After I got off the couch, just barely, I crawled my way up the stairs. I needed to put on some clothes to be presentable for the white people down in the office. They already thought I didn't have a lick of sense, which wasn't completely true. Even though I could show out. I wouldn't be doing that today. I'd be playing the role of nice, sophisticated Luna, or shit, begging ass Luna if I needed to to try and keep them off my back for now.

I went into my room and opened my closet door. I figured a t-shirt and a pair of jeans would be suitable, that way I looked like I was having a normal day, which I was, except the fact that I was also hurt as fuck between the legs. So, I'd have to figure out a way to keep myself on my toes.

If Stone were here, I bet he'd carry me. I smiled at my thought, but that was a crazy way of thinking, especially since I had no way of getting in contact with him. He didn't even leave me his phone number, but come to think of it, he didn't even seem like he had a phone. Not that I cared, but it would've been nice for him to take my number anyway. He could've used a payphone or somebody else's phone to get in contact with me. Maybe he had another woman or women. Who knows at this point? What a gentleman too. When I fell asleep last night, I dreamt about his body and what it would be like to lay on him all night. Just for the time that I was in his lap, I felt like it was where I belonged. I had never been more comfortable anywhere else than I was in his lap, but I would probably never see him again. If I did, I didn't antici-pate it would be any time soon. I could always ask Black since he was looking for him in the first place, and maybe play

Devil's Advocate that way, but there was no telling if that would work.

Shaking the thoughts of Stone out of my mind, I put my clothes on, slid on my shoes, and grabbed my papers from the hospital in case this would give me some type of sympathy and headed out the door. I thought about taking a few of my pain pills, but that wouldn't do anything but knock me out, something I didn't want to have happen, so I just kept on going. Down the sidewalk, as always, the housing authority just looked like they were ready to take somebodies money. Looking like they can't wait to see you break the bank to live in a fucking project. I honestly couldn't be more embarrassed, because Link's fucking checks bounced, so I wondered what was even going on with that. The last time I checked, he had plenty of money, and there would be no reason for it, but I would probably never know that either. This was going to be the day of forever unanswered questions.

Someone was coming out of the office as I was coming in with tears running down their face.

"Don't go in there. They're fucking terrible!" The woman sniffled, and I knew I had gotten myself into the wrong shit.

"Lawd, if you can hear me, please, please don't make my crazy come out, because then I'm going to lose my home, and we both know what will happen then. Be an electric fence!"

I prayed before stepping all the way into the office. Right in front, behind the protected glass, yes, I'm saying protected because I've seen many people show their asses in this office, was Ms. Penelope, the lady that sent me the message in the first place. She had a nameplate sitting on her desk that made the whole office seem too serious. Like, you've got this giant ass glass window like you're a bank and the nameplate? I cannot take this woman seriously.

Luckily, there wasn't a line, and I was the only person, besides Ms. Penelope who was in the office.

"Hello, Ms. Penelope, my name is Luna Baker, and I just wanted to come and talk to you about my rent situation."

"Situation?" she asked, looking over her glasses like she didn't understand me.

"Yes, ma'am. I received a text letting me know that the last two checks for my account had bounced, and I wanted to try and negotiate the money portion. Perhaps I could pay half now, and then pay as the days go on till I get back caught up."

A smile appeared on her face, and it was the most wicked smile I'd ever seen. She placed her index finger up to the glass and turned her back to walk away. This woman couldn't have been more than one hundred and ten pounds soaking wet, and she had on stockings. It was at least ninety degrees outside, but you know what, get it how you live because it's your life...all day, but don't act stuck up or like I'm asking for something impossible.

When she came back, she had a manila-looking file with my name on it. She set it down and cracked it open, reading it like it was a book. She slid her little pasty finger down the front paper and scanned it with her granny glasses that hung from pearls.

"Mmm.....I see here you've never been late and haven't had any other issues besides this one here. Unfortunately, since you've had not one but two checks bounce, we'll only be able to accept cash or money order from you from here on out, but I think the half payment should be just fine. When do you expect to be paying the rest?"

"Well, I've been in the hospital the last two days, and I don't get paid till next week, so I've missed a few days of working. I won't know what my check plus tips looks like for another few days, but if it's allowed, I can call back up here when I know and let you know. I'm prepared to make the first payment today."

"Excellent, you'll need to do so in order to hold off on the eviction."

Just hearing the word eviction made my skin crawl, like what? I didn't want to even think about getting evicted. That just meant I had to work even harder for the next couple of days to hopefully be able to get caught up and prepare for the next week to pay more rent. I didn't know how I was going to do it, but I had faith that it was going to go well, or at least I hoped.

I grabbed the money I had placed in my jean pocket before leaving the house and handed it to the lady. There was no need for me to keep any of the money Black gave me. I knew I needed it all, and I gave it all too little Ms. Penelope because I didn't want this coming back to haunt me.

She pulled out a pen and her receipt pad, signed my receipt, and stuck it out the small, hand only hole to give to me.

"Good luck, Ms. Baker."

"Thank you," I said before turning my back to walk away. I couldn't say just yet, but I hoped this would work out in my favor. At least this was one thing off my damn back, but that still left my car. I knew me getting my car fixed wasn't going to happen right now or probably any time soon if I'm being honest, but I'd have to figure out how I was going to get around because walking to and from work wasn't going to work—not until I healed anyway. I didn't even have any more money for a Lyft or anything. Why didn't I just at least keep twenty dollars? I was not being smart, even though I was trying to be responsible.

I still had seven hours before I had to be at work, so I figured I'd lay back down and think some more about Stone, and how last night with him reminded me of what it was like to be treated like a lady and not a common whore.

❧ II ❧

PANDORA

I honestly hated bittersweet moments like this. Finally, fina-fucking-ly, I was about to be with the man of not only my dreams but my destiny. Since my conception, Stone was practically chosen for me, to be my mate, my man, the one to spend the rest of my days with, and I was ok with that. I had fallen for him easily, who wouldn't? He was good to look at, great in bed, and it just felt right with him, but what I couldn't understand was why he wasn't into me like I was him. Even when we had sex, I could feel there was no connection. He was only screwing me so that he could have sex because none of the other female gargoyles would dare touch him knowing he belonged to me, not unless they wanted to lose a finger, hand, or their life.

Last night was the first night, well, the only night that Stone didn't come home and I didn't know where he was. He said he was going to talk to Black, but I didn't think that would take all night. At the rate our people were falling ill, and to their deaths, I would have thought he would want to get back in a hurry, or at least be here with his comrades to mourn the loss of their queen, or to help spread the word, something, but he wasn't here, which meant one thing, that he must've been hurt. The only reason I didn't think he was in any trouble was because I would have felt it unless he was in so much trouble that he was unable to.

I had never gone to bed without first knowing what was going on with Stone, and this worried me. The sun was falling in the human world, so it would be safe for me to enter without turning to stone. I just hoped I found him in enough time and in no trouble or pain.

Luckily for me, I'd already had a shower for the day and was dressed for whatever. I could fight in anything need be, but I wanted to blend in with the people just in case I had to go on some weird search for him. I figured he'd be at the bar, or he'd at least eventually turn up, and I didn't want to be sitting in there looking crazy or out of place in something uptight or even my semi-royal robes.

There was an off the shoulder powder blue dress I'd been wanting to wear with my nude thong flip-flops. I had a hand-made beaded flower that would match the dress and silver accessories to offset the entire outfit. I never wore my dreads up. My face, to me, was shaped funny, and I hated the way it looked with my hair up, so I always wore it down.

Even as a gargoyle, I'm a fairly normal woman. I want my man and everything that should be mine, and that's all. I don't want anything extra, and nothing more or less.

As I was about to leave the suite I shared with Stone, I opened the door and ran straight into my mother, who was standing in my doorway looking at me strangely.

"Pandora, what are you doing? Why are you dressed like that?"

"Relax, mother, I'm trying to go check on Stone. He didn't come back last night, and I want to make sure he's ok and that everything went smoothly with Black."

"Little girl let me tell you something, you need to hook,

line, and sink this man. Wherever he is, however he moves, is the way you should as well. You need to be there every step of the way. As the future queen, you will have your hands in business affairs as well. Change your clothes; you're revealing too much."

I looked down at myself as my mother further criticized my clothes and the way I looked, and even though I heard her, I had to tune her out. My mother and I had often been accused of being twins, sisters, instead of mother and daughter. She was hard on me, very hard. I learned to fight early, how to be a "lady" early, and here's a fun fact, I'm not just Pandora, I'm a princess, though I hated for people to call me that. In the beginning, before there was just one set of a king and queen, there were four, to rule over the four gargoyle clans. My father was the king of the Rose clan before he passed away, and since he had no male heir, we were overrun, overtaken, and I was sent here with my mother, to the closest kingdom to seek refuge from King Kairo and Queen Zaya. I always wondered before why I was never paired with anyone from our clan, but when I became of age, my mother told me it was because I was meant for greater things, that being a princess meant aligning ourselves with gargoyles who were higher up on the food chain, and it didn't get any higher than Stone.

Though the king and queen never called him their son, we all knew how close he was to them and that one day, it would be his duty to take over. Now it was finally going to be happening, and I would rule happily by his side for at least the next six or seven centuries. Without another royal to marry in our kingdom, there was no point in staying around, at least not to my mother. Otherwise, she would've kept me in a corrupt kingdom, but instead, she brought us to safety where Queen Zaya and King Kairo graciously made Stone my true mate, and they couldn't have done anything greater.

"Hello, Pandora, do you hear me?" My mother snapped her fingers at me.

"Yes, mother. I hear you. Unfortunately, I have to get going. Just because you don't like my clothes doesn't mean Stone doesn't. He doesn't have a problem with the way I dress, so neither should you."

I tried my hardest to slide past her, but she yanked me by my arm pulling me back into the room.

"Mother, what is your problem today?"

"You. You're not taking this seriously. You live in a fantasy world where you believe in love, and while that is beautiful, that's not realistic. The throne is yours, and you need to take that seriously. Keep in mind what it will mean to be a queen. You should start dressing like it, talking like it, and acting like it. Do you understand?"

"Yes, now let me go!" I shouted, rattling the walls of the suite. I had somewhat of a temper and was the wrong one to fuck with, even my mother knew not to push or tempt me too far. I was dressed fine, and she was being a little too old school for me. Even in the realm, that didn't stop the years and fashion sense from progressing, and as time goes on, so must we.

I finally made it out of her grasp and ran outside at full speed to get up the momentum to get through the barrier. When I made it through, thank goodness it was already dark, and not about to be. That could've been a bad situation. I stood as still as possible, trying to feel where Stone was, and I could sense that he was nearby. The only place I knew he knew about, and barely knew anything about it in the first place, was Bar Scovel, so I headed in that direction, hoping to find him to get answers and prepare for the mating ritual.

❧ 12 ❧

STONE

It was rare that I slept inside of my wings. Normally, I kept them in or only halfway out, but for some reason, I needed to be embraced. It had been a very long time since I held a woman and enjoyed it. Holding Pandora sometimes made me want to get out of bed and leave completely because I hated lying next to her. She would wrap her leg around me, and it just didn't feel like anything. I know it should have, but it didn't. If anything, when she laid on me, it only struck a nerve or anger. I was only two seconds away from hating Pandora. I didn't want to be king; that was crazy to me, especially because Black's clan was supposed to be getting on the throne now.

But, when I woke up, my mind immediately went to Luna and what she might be doing. I figured she might still be asleep, since it was only just a little after six, and though I wanted to see her, I would look crazy coming to see her in the same clothes I had on, and I didn't want to go all the way back to the realm to change and risk running into Pandora because I knew she'd try to tag along with me. I hated giving her orders—she was too eager to please all the damn time.

One thing I had never done while being in the human world was shop, even though we had money for emergencies. Anything could happen, but I hadn't even thought to bring any money with me, so now I was going to have to steal like some common thief. I didn't even know where to go to do something like that, but I figured if I headed back toward town, I could find somewhere to get a few things, to clean myself up a bit. I didn't need a full blown shower, but a little wash-up and some new clothes wouldn't hurt.

I jumped from the roof and landed directly on my feet behind the buildings Luna lived in. I wanted to knock on the door and ask to see her, but now didn't seem like the right time, so I just kept it moving, and if it wasn't too late, then I could go back and check on her. Something about her had me wanting to get to know more about her, and I hoped she would let me, but in reality, I needed to keep this to myself because there was nothing I could really do with her; she was human after all, but there wasn't anything wrong with trying to find a friend.

As I strolled into town, I felt a very familiar presence, and the scent was strong. I had just passed by Bar Scovel, and if I didn't know any better, I would think Pandora was inside, but I couldn't worry about her right now. I was on a mission to get some clothes so I could go on about my business the way I had intended to the night before.

The nightlife was in rare form, and there were lots of people on the streets and standing in front of the stores, which made it easy to disguise what I was about to do. There were so many shops on the corners and squeezed in between bars, it was nothing to grab what I needed and keep it moving. There was a Joe's Crab Shack right behind one of the bars where there was an entire outfit just calling out to me. I didn't need new shoes or anything, just the clothes them-selves, so I waited till I thought nobody was looking and snuck in and grabbed a shirt and a pair of the beach shorts they had near the door and stepped back out like I was never there. It was crazy; humans were so careless, so reckless, they never paid attention to anything going on around them and thought everything was hunky dory when it couldn't have been further from that. There were people all over the world wondering why they didn't have powers or couldn't see the supernatural, and it's because of the lack of being able to see, to truly see what's there in their faces. It isn't so much what you can't see but what you choose to see. Opening your mind can do a hell of a lot for you if you want it to.

At the end of the road, there was a closed alleyway, so I used it to take off my clothes and put on new ones. I didn't think too well about the damn plan I had with my clothes. I was gonna have to throw out my old clothes because I couldn't be walking around time with them nor could I show up on Luna's doorstep with them in my hands. I didn't want to look homeless because I was living like a king, literally, not that Luna cared about any of that. I could tell she was a down to earth kind of girl and that she worried about her own house, but she shouldn't, because I had my own, and I could care less about what she had going on. I mean just in that aspect.

Enough of that soft shit, anyway, I put on the new clothes and headed back towards Luna. I had never been nervous about really doing anything, except for losing the king and queen; that's the first time I can remember being worried about something, but this, I was worried for a different reason. I wasn't supposed to be getting hung up with a human, and Luna did something like cast a spell on me last night without doing anything at all.

She was so open and transparent, and she didn't have an ulterior motive in getting to know me. She didn't care where I was from, which was perfect for me, because from what I could tell, humans were all about the glitz and glam of life and didn't know how to appreciate the things that were right in front of them, but Luna did; I could tell. She took pride in her home, it looked like everything I would imagine she would want, and I loved that she had her taste.

Pandora was a yes girl, and she did as she was told. She wore the things I liked, not the things she wanted, not really. She didn't even have her brain, and I wanted a woman who could think for herself.

By the time I got back over to Luna's, it was about seven-thirty, and I didn't know if she'd be home or awake, or if she'd even feel like being bothered. I didn't wanna force myself into her life, but I wanted to be around her, at least for now, while I was in the human world. I had time to kill since the other gargoyles were probably getting themselves together, especially Black who owned a business, so he was more than likely getting himself together for the evening. I was trying to convince myself of that shit too. I didn't want to say that I just wanted to see Luna first, because afterwards, I would probably never, ever see her again.

I walked up the short walkway to her house and knocked on the door. Standing there, I wondered if she'd look out the window to check and see who it was before she just snatched the door open, but she didn't. This was what I meant by careless. They were too damn trusting, fucking humans.

"Stone? How are you? What are you doing here?" she asked through the screen portion of her door. "I'm good. I just wanted to see you before I handled my business with Black and then went home. I don't know if I'll get to catch up with you after this, so I wanted to say thank you for last night, for listening to me."

"It's no problem, why don't you come on in? I don't have to be at work for a few hours. We can hang out here."

She unlocked the lock on the screen door, and I pulled it open using the handle.

"Are you hungry? I just finished making fried chicken, mashed potatoes, macaroni, and turnip greens. You're more than welcome to anything you'd like."

My eyebrow went up when she said anything I'd like. It was like my primal instinct to just fuck her silly kept popping in my head, and no matter how hard I forced it down, it just wouldn't go away, but I needed to sit down at the table so my hard-on wouldn't get to her, even though I wanted to give it to her.

"I'd love some, thanks for offering."

She led me to the table and uncovered the food. I thought it was crazy that she had all of this food for just herself.

"You made this for just yourself? This is a lot of food, Luna."

"Seems like it, doesn't it? It's actually my mother's favorite meal, and I made it for her, but she said she wasn't really hungry, and she can't handle all of this food on her stomach since she takes her chemo treatments, so more food for me I guess."

Though she wore a smile on her face, from the way she bounced around, I could tell she was uncomfortable. She was fidgeting around, moving the serving plates around on the table, trying to make my plate for me.

"Woah, whoa, Luna, you don't have to make my plate; I'm a grown man, I can make it myself."

"No, you're a guest, I can make it for you, don't worry."

I just nodded my head. I could see her mother was a sore subject, and I didn't want to add to the pain, but I also didn't want her tip-toeing around the issue, whether she was talking to me or not.

Gently, I grabbed her wrist, holding it firmly but not roughly. "Luna, slow down and look at me."

Like a robot, she stopped in her place and turned to face me. "What's the matter, Stone?"

"You tell me. You mention your mother taking chemo, and then boom, you're moving all around the kitchen. If you wanna talk about it, then talk about it. Don't force yourself to because you're around a stranger, ok?"

Tears welled up in her eyes, and I could tell I pushed a few buttons she wasn't used to having pushed. I wondered where her friends were or maybe even a boyfriend. Where was the man who knocked her up?

I pulled her closer to me and into my lap, and she put her head on mine.

"Listen to me, your mother is the woman who gave birth to you, and if you want to talk about what's going on with her, then do it. If you want to talk about this procedure you had, then talk about it. You can't be nervous to say certain things because you think other people don't want to hear it or that you're sharing too much information. I'm in your house, so you must trust me somewhat. I watched you sleep last night, carried you on my back, and covered you up. I'm not a stranger...I'm a friend."

I felt the side of my face getting wet from the tears she was crying, and I moved my head to wipe her tears away. I know this is going to sound terrible, but it was something beautiful about a woman's tears. Not when she was all snotted up, but when she had lone tears falling from her eyes like they were raindrops, it was a beautiful disaster, and that's what Luna was.

"I'm sorry, Stone, you're right. I need to empty it out, but I didn't want to do that to you because you don't know me, and I don't want to chase you off so easily. You seem like a nice guy, but I don't know. I've been fooled before."

"You very well may have, but I can guarantee you don't know anybody else like me, and that's a promise. So, tell me, where is the person you're supposed to count on? Where is the father of the baby you lost?"

Luna reached up and put her hands in my hair and began combing her fingers through it as she spoke. "Link was what I thought was the love of my life. He was very important to me, but he had several other lives that I didn't know about until two years later, and when I told him I was pregnant, he was already gone. He never even cared really. I haven't heard from him since I told him I was pregnant, and then I lost the baby, so...I don't know where he is."

"And how do you feel about that, honestly?"

She sat there for a moment as if she were truly thinking it through, and then, she took a deep breath.

"Honestly, I'm mad, and I want to know who the fuck he thinks he is leaving me like that. On top of that, my mother and her chemo treatments, that was something he used to help me with. He would go with her to them sometimes, and sometimes we'd go together. I haven't even told her I was pregnant, had a miscarriage, or that we even broke up. It's just a lot to deal with, and then my boss, Black, he gets on my nerves on another level. Like, what type of man would make you still work even when you're pretty much weak at the knees and can barely stand up?

That's crazy!"

Hearing her say that about Black instantly frustrated me, and I hoped I heard her wrong.

"Can you say that again? What did you say about Black?"

"Yeah, I mean, I know you said you have business with him, but he's an asshole and treats his employees like crap, especially me, mostly me, and I'm tired of working there. I wanna throw away the whole life."

I didn't mean to laugh, but I couldn't help it.

Throwing away life as if it were her own to toss aside.

"One thing at a time. If you hate your job, find another one. You're a beautiful girl, I can't imagine why anyone wouldn't want you working with them, and you're a great conversationalist, good host. If this Link dude didn't treat you like a queen, you didn't need to have him around you, because you deserve better. Now come on, let's eat this food before it gets cold, so I can see if you cook better than you made that Kool-Aid last night."

"OH, YOU GOT JOKE JOKES, COOL!"

She rose from my lap and walked to the other side of the table, and we both dug into our food, eating like it was our last supper.

13

LUNA

A few hours later, we were still just sitting at the table laughing and talking. I loved being able to open up to Stone because the truth was I didn't have one friend. I mean, not a damn one. How would I? I dropped out of high school early, the only job I had was working at the bar, and that was at night. The only people I knew were men, and they all just wanted to smash, but not Stone. He was kind, and sweet, and he could tell a good joke, and I really liked being able to laugh, especially since I felt like I was sad all the damn time. Depression is real, and sometimes, it really does just come in waves. It wasn't something that I felt all the time, but every now and then, it fucked with me.

"So, judging by the way you just raw dogged your food, I'ma say you liked it way better than the Kool-
Aid."

"Waaayyyyy better. You did a good job. I could use a meal like that more often."

"Then why don't you have one? I'm sure you have a lady waiting for you wherever you're from."

For a second, I thought I sensed hesitation in him. I saw

his face and how he looked at me. I just got up from the table and started clearing it, because soon, I would have to go to work, and we'd been sitting here too long already. I began gathering the plates, and he stood to help me get the dishes from his side. I didn't even look at him, because I was wondering when he was going to say something or what he would say if he did say anything at all, and then when I thought we'd be in silence for the rest of the time he was there, he said something.

"I don't have a girlfriend or a wife, or anything like that. I have no children, no baby mama, none of that, but you know I told you about my parents who kind of try to tell me what to do? To live like them? Well, I have someone in my life they've tried to set me up with, and we have messed around a bit, but I'm not really into her. She's not my type. When I'm with her, I don't feel anything, like nothing, and I've never been in love, but I know it should feel good, it should feel like...I don't know, but it couldn't possibly feel like what it does with her."

"Mmm...so...does she know you feel this way about her, or does she think you have feelings for her? Are you leading her on?"

"Hell no. I have told her from the beginning how I truly feel, and if I could, I would get rid of her. I've tried to give her to someone else, but nobody will take her, and she follows me around all the time. I don't know, Luna, it's complicated."

"Perhaps you could make it simple if you wanted. Remember what we just talked about yesterday? Doing what you want to live your life and make yourself happy? You've only got one life to live, stop wasting it on making other people happy."

Now, let me be honest, I said that because he needed to hear it, but also because I couldn't deny the feelings between us. I don't wanna hear anybody's mouth about it only being

86

one night because most of y'all bitches will meet a man and bring him back to your house that same night and smash, and then have to chase after him. It ain't nothin' wrong with what

I'm doing because I'm not giving up the pum-pum.

I'm just chilling and relaxing, enjoying this fine chocolate curly-fro'd man!

"You're right. That's actually what I came to talk to Black about, kind of. I need to have a discussion with him that could change everything for me in a good way. You think he'll be in tonight?"

"Yeah, let me text him to make sure, but I'm pretty sure he will be."

I finished putting the dishes in the sink and grabbed my phone and sent Black a text making sure he was coming in for the night and waited for him to respond, which he never did.

"Ok, I need to get ready for work. Uhm, you know where the remote is if you want to watch TV, there's more food if you get hungry, and uhm. I guess you can relax unless you want me to walk you out before I go upstairs."

"Why would I be leaving you? I'm walking you to work. I assumed since I didn't see your car out front that you didn't get it fixed yet. It's way too late for you to be walking anywhere by yourself, so when you're ready, we'll leave together. Not like I'm not going there anyway."

I was standing at the bottom of the stairs, and as I was talking, Stone was coming in my direction, and I had to brace myself. The way he moved made me feel like he was my man, like he belonged here, in my presence, with me only. I had to try not to get too used to that, especially knowing now that he had some girl who was hanging onto him, even if he wasn't hanging onto her. That shit fucked me up, but there wasn't anything I could do about it. I didn't know anything about Stone, and the things I did know, they were surface things. I didn't know how old he was, where he was from, anything like that, but I couldn't deny the connection I felt when we were together, whether I knew him or not. I just hoped he wasn't a rapist or a murderer, but he couldn't be as protective over me he was being.

Stone put his hand around my waist and pulled me close to him, our bodies were touching, and my pussy began to ache from more than just a miscarriage. I wanted him to touch me, but I couldn't let him. I would get an infection for sure, and that shit would be nasty.

"Luna, go get ready for work. I'll be right here when you get done."

Stone bent down and kissed me on the cheek, and where he left his lips, I could feel heat surging through my face. His lips were soft and moist; even after the kiss was over, I could still feel it.

Normally, I would run up the stairs, but I could hardly move. I had to drag myself up to my room to get ready because I wanted him so badly, but I knew that wasn't going to happen right now.

From upstairs, I listened downstairs, to see if he turned on the television, and from what I could tell, he hadn't. It seemed like he hadn't even moved. I wanted to yell down to him to ask if he was ok, but I figured that would make me stall more, and I didn't want to be late to work. I had already showered, so I brushed my teeth, washed my face, put on more deodorant and body spray, and then put on my black leather leggings with a pink crop top. It was Friday, and that meant the bar would be jumping. Register or not, I might still get some tips just for looking good, and with the predicament, I was in financially, I needed all the money I could get.

I looked at myself in the mirror, worrying what Stone might think or what he might say, and I felt unsure of myself. I wondered if he would like what I had on or if he thought I was doing too much. I'd have to wait and see. I grabbed my purse and wallet, my house keys and phone were downstairs, and so was Stone. He was just too good to be true, or at least that's what it seemed like.

Going down the stairs, I said a silent prayer over myself. I just wanted to go to work and get this night over with, so I could come home and get in bed and daydream about a life that I'd never be able to have. Stone seemed so perfect, and I just wondered how he was so wonderful. Where did he come from? He was...just amazing.

"Stone, you ready to go?" I put my purse around my shoulder and grabbed my keys off the ring. "Can you grab my phone off the charger too?"

"Of course."

In my mind, this was what normal couples did; they said bye to each other. They walked each other to the car or had sweet goodbyes. It was crazy that I felt so strongly about a complete stranger, one that I might not ever see again, and that was the worst part. I was having entirely too much fun with someone I may never see again.

With my phone in his hand, he walked back into the living room and looked at me with a strange expression.

"What's the matter?"

"Nothing's wrong, I'm just wondering why you've got that little ass shirt on."

"You don't like it?" I asked, looking down at the shirt, pulling it down a little.

"I do like it, I just don't want nobody else seeing you in it."

"Seriously, Stone?"

"I'm dead ass. I don't like—"

His words were cut off, and he reached for his rib like he was in pain. "Stone, what's wrong?"

❧ 14 ❧

STONE

Everything was fine until I saw her in that little bitty ass shirt, and something happened in me. Something in me changed. I had never had this feeling before, well, maybe once during battle, but other than that, I hadn't experienced this feeling.

"Stone, what's wrong?" I heard her repeat herself, and I had to bend over to keep her from seeing my eyes; I knew they were changing. I could feel the heat inside of me raging like a bull runs towards a cape. This emotion I was feeling was jealousy, I think. Maybe it was envy, for the men who would be watching her tonight in a crowded bar, especially knowing the men in there would more than likely all be gargoyles. I couldn't handle the thought of something like that. It would be some gargoyles gettin' killed tonight if everybody wasn't careful.

"I'm...ok." I all but roared. I had to figure out how to get my emotions in check, especially over a woman that didn't even belong to me, who after tonight, I would not lay eyes on again.

"Stone..." Luna reached her hand out for me, and I turned

around. I couldn't figure out how to get the gargoyle in me to be quiet and lay down. This fool was going to get us exposed, but after a minute or so, he calmed down, and I could feel my gray, ashen eyes go back inside of themselves, and everything was ok, at least for now. I turned back around to see a worried look on Luna's face.

"I'm ok, don't worry. I think it was just gas or somethin'. It'll pass, but no, I don't like that shirt."

"Well, you gon' have to deal with it. This shirt is going to make me some extra money- why am I explaining myself to you? Boy, come on if you're still walking me to work. I don't want to be late, and Black text back and said he's already at work."

She turned around and walked toward the door and almost slammed the door in my face.

Damn, she was legit mad as fuck, and she kind of told me about myself, something I wasn't used to, not really. Pandora was snappy with women, but never with me, not once, and I liked that shit, and for once, I followed after a woman.

Luna was speed walking down the sidewalk; she didn't even lock her damn door because she was stomping off. I was letting this woman get me caught up in my feelings so much that I was starting to think I was human myself.

"Luna, Luna, I'm sorry!" I yelled out to her, using my gargoyle vibes to stop her in her tracks. She was stuck and didn't even know it. Literally, her body stopped where it was, and she couldn't move even if she wanted to. I had powers that even I forgot about sometimes.

I caught up to her at the end of the sidewalk and stood in front of her.

"Listen, I'm sorry. I've never seen that kind of shirt before. It just seems a little short. I understand the job you have, and what you do, so I'm sorry for misunderstanding and talking to you like a child. You're a grown ass woman and can wear whatever you want."

She crossed her arms for a second, wanting to be mad, but then she dropped them right beside her and let out a deep sigh. I felt it was safe to let her move again on her own.

"No, I'm sorry. I didn't mean to go all ghetto girl on you. Forgive me?"

"Always, now come on so you won't be late."

The night before, we held hands home from her job, and tonight, we held hands on the way. It was still new, but it was something I liked. I liked the way her hand tingled in mine when our fingers touched one another.

The walk was somewhat silent, but before we got to the door, Luna grabbed my arm and turned me to face her.

"What's wrong, Luna?"

"Nothing...nothing is wrong per say, but what happens after tonight? Do you go back to your life, wherever that is, or...what? I mean, I've enjoyed having you around me the last day or so, and from what I can see, you don't have a phone...so..."

"Will me getting a phone help? I will have to go back home, but I guess a phone could help us both."

"If you wouldn't normally have a phone, then you don't have to get one for me, but if you just want a phone then—"

I grabbed her face and kissed her. She was talking so much, and she just needed to relax. I was feeling the same way she was, and I could tell she was afraid to ask me what I was thinking or what I wanted, but I wasn't the type of gargoyle to play games. I went after what I wanted, even though this was totally new to me considering she was human but human or not, I couldn't lie and say the connection wasn't growing or that it didn't exist.

Luna put her arms around my neck, standing on her toes to meet my kiss, to kiss me the way I was trying to kiss her.

Up against the door, I could feel her leg finding its way up my body, and I wanted her legs around my waist. I wanted to feel the heat between those legs, so I lifted her up and spun her around, making her hit her back against the wall.

"Ohhh!" she yelled, our parts only separating for just a second.

My hand slid up her back, and hers onto mine, rubbing my shoulder blades. I realized something though. This never happened with Pandora, and I guess it was because she wasn't really what I wanted, but the more aroused I became, the more I felt my wings about to spread out, so as much as I wanted to continue this kiss, it had to stop.

I pulled away from her, and her lips were still in mid-kiss.

"What's...the...matter?" she asked me in between breaths.

"Everything's right...I promise, see." I grabbed one of her hands and put it on my pants, where she could feel the print of my dick beating against my pants, begging to come out. Luna had me riled up, and I don't care what type of sex she had before. Until you've been fucked by a gargoyle, you ain't talkin' 'bout nothin'.

"Mmmm..I see. Well, then we should stop."

"Yes, we should."

I kissed the inside of her neck and put her down. She began fixing her shirt and her clothes, making sure her stuff that was in her purse was still there, and once she realized everything was ok, she smoothed out her clothes, kissed me on the cheek, and gave me a wink, going in before me.

I don't know what I'm getting myself into, but I hope it's something I don't have to get myself out of.

❧ 15 ❧

PANDORA

I'd been in this bar for hours waiting on Stone to show up. I knew he would at some point, I could feel it, but I didn't know when, until now. There was something happening with him on the other side of the door, I could feel the excitement in his body, but I didn't know what it was from. That was the only thing I hated about not being completely mated—I couldn't read his as well. But once we completely mated, I'd be able to feel him and know what was going on, and I couldn't wait for that to happen.

The door to the bar flung open, and there was a girl who walked in that went directly behind the bar and sat in a chair behind the register. Other than myself, she was the only female in here. I'd crossed paths with another before coming in, but that was it. Seemed like it was a man's world almost, but women made the world go round, literally. We give life!

Whoever this girl was, there were a few things I didn't like about her. I didn't care how cute she was, there was no reason she should be smelling like Stone. She had his scent all over her, and it made me want to puke. She was pretty, but she wasn't me. I'm a princess; she seemed like some common human, who clearly had no wealth, no title, no...nothing it seemed. When she came over to me, I almost fainted because of how strongly she smelled of MY man.

"Hi, welcome to Bar Scovel, have you been helped already?" she asked with a smile on her face.

I looked her up and down, sizing her up, trying to see what she was about.

"No, I'm fine. I'm waiting on my boyfriend to join me. I believe he's right outside."

"Oh, ok, well I'm Luna. If you need anything, give me a shout."

"Will do."

I rolled my eyes and turned around, facing the crowd, waiting for Stone to come in. When he did, his scent hit me like a ton of bricks, something I was used to, but it was now mixed in with this Luna's. Their scents danced in one another, and I could smell arousal on both of them. They smelled like one another. Surely he wasn't having sex with a human. What was this?

I turned back around and saw Stone coming in with a smile on his face—that was something that was already irregular. I had never seen him smile this much, and not at a woman. His eyes were all over Luna, and she was following his smile around the bar.

"Can I get you something to drink?" she asked.

"Nah, I'm good. Black around?"

"I don't know, we both just got here, remember?
Let me go in the back and see."

Luna headed to the back, and someone threw a glass at the bar, landing right in front of her. Stone was over to her in milliseconds, rushing to her to make sure she didn't hit the ground. When I saw his hands on her and how he held her, I almost passed

out. I could feel the love and lust pulsating through him.

How did he know this woman? Why was he pushing up on her like this? Ultimately, I, of course, wondered what she had that I didn't. Perhaps this was just some kind of adventure for him. He couldn't possibly want her, could he?

His big arms embraced her and pulled her into his chest. He then moved her back in front of himself, inspecting each inch of her body like she'd been hit, when that wasn't the case, not even a little bit.

"Stone!" I called out to him. We had bigger things to focus on, like Black, and not his little human almost getting hit by a broken glass.

He waved me off and followed behind Luna to the back. This was something that had never happened before, and I'd never been so upset. Who was he shoeing off like I was nobody? I know it couldn't have been me, but instead of showing out or acting out, I did what I thought my mother would tell me to do, and that was follow behind him. Soon, he would be king, and I would be the queen, and I didn't always have to have my way, but I should always support my king, and that's what I was going to do.

I left the crowded, loud bar and headed into the hallway where I saw them disappear, and they were pushed up one another on the wall, kissing passionately. Not like they were about to fuck, but like...there was something between them. Stone never kissed me like that. He never cared for me like that. A part of me wondered if I was finally losing my mind because there was no way this could be happening, not right in my face.

"Stone, what are you doing?"

Almost as if he didn't care, he pulled away from Luna and walked over to me. "Pandora, what are you doing back here?"

"Answer my question first. What are you doing here, with her?"

"With her? My name is Luna, just to remind you." "Don't talk to me, human!" I seethed.

"Human, you're human too. What, was that supposed to be a shot?" Luna rolled her eyes with a smile.

"That's enough. Luna, this is Pandora, Pandora, this is Luna. Now, Pandora, why are you here?"

"I came to help you, to support you, but I find you here, with her, doing...something you know you shouldn't be doing. You should be focused on Black, and then we can go home to get things in order for the funeral."

"And I am focused. I've never been more focused, and I don't need you here standing over my shoulder to make sure I get things done. You need to leave."

I couldn't believe what I was hearing. For centuries, we'd known each other, and he was pushing me out, for what? A human? That couldn't be it; there had to be more to the story.

"I'm not leaving. It is my duty to stand by your side. We're meant to be together, remember?" I tried to brush my fingers against his face so that he could remember my touch, but he grabbed my wrist before it could even touch him.

"Go home, Pandora. Don't make me tell you again!"

I saw the gray behind his eyes threatening to come out, and I didn't want to test him, not in here, and make him ruin what was to be. I could keep my cool, long enough to get home, but when I got there, there was no telling what I was going to do. Not only was I mad, but I was hurt.

Yes, I know he doesn't love me, but when you've devoted yourself, your life, everything you are to another person, and they won't do the same for you, it's painful to watch, and to see that person with someone else is even worse.

"Why? Go home, why, so you can be with your little human?"

"PANDORA!"

Stone grabbed my arms and pushed me up against the wall, holding my wrists tightly.

"Stone, stop, you're going to hurt her!" Luna yelled, and it was to my surprise. Why was she trying to defend me, someone, she didn't even know?"

"Luna, back up. I'm sick of this shit. Pandora, go home, and I'll join you there when I get back. You have no right to tell me to do anything, and you know this. From this moment on, I want to make it clear, we're done, and I'm tired of living a life according to what other people say I should. Now, leave!" He released my wrists before leaving me standing there hurt and confused. Luna shook her head as if she were upset as well, and I couldn't figure out why. I had never felt so threatened by anyone before, especially not a human, and now I was going to lose my man to one? That didn't make any sense, but I would leave, for now, go back to the realm and plan out my next idea. If I couldn't get to him with a sexy dress that he didn't even notice, or by trying to keep him focused on the whole reason he came, I'd have to try a different approach. I needed to speak to my mother—the only person who would know what to do in this situation.

❦ 16 ❦

LUNA

Stone snatched away from Pandora forcefully, and of course, I didn't know him, but it seemed out of his nature to be rough with a woman. He was always so gentle with me, but it had only been a day. There was no telling what was going on under there.

Stone was in the corner of the hallway with his hands over his face, like he was thinking or perhaps beating himself up over what happened, and I felt horrible. I knew what it was like to lose control, and I hated that he was feeling anything other than happy since he was in such a good mood right before that.

I reached out to him, and he accepted my touch. We didn't know shit about one another, but that Pandora, I could tell she was the one he was telling me about earlier. There were so many questions I had, but I figured now wasn't the time to ask them, and in due time, all things reveal themselves.

"You wanna talk about it?" I asked, putting my head up against his chest.

"Not really, I do need to be talking to Black. She was right, I need to focus."

"And I'm a distraction?"

"No, of course not, that's not what I'm saying. You almost got hit by glass, and that would've been bad. You would've been bleeding, so of course, I didn't want to see anything bad happen to you, and we got in the hallway and just got carried away. You're not a distraction, you could never be, no matter what, but I do need to go in here with a clear mind and do this alone." He stroked my dreads that were up in a bun, of course, and I was just surprised by how quickly things were moving, but it felt...right, not like it was forced.

"I understand. He should be in his office, just knock first. He can't stand somebody who just walks in."

Stone pulled away from me and looked down at me and smiled before kissing me on my forehead. As I was walking away, I saw him open the door, without knocking. That man was a world of trouble, and I just knew it, but I didn't care, not really. I wanted to keep him around me because he made me feel good and safe. I guess he must've been good at his security job.

17

STONE

I wasn't going to knock. Even though I wanted peace, I wasn't willing to kiss his ass to have it. That wasn't going to happen. I walked right in, ready to get down to business, but I knew it wasn't going to be that easy.

"You must have a death wish coming in here like this, in my place of business AGAIN, thinking I owe you something."

"I hear all of that bull you're spouting, but we have bigger things to worry about, and I've come to try and discuss them with you like a civilized gargoyle, instead of a rogue savage," I said as I sat down in the seat on the other side of his desk, propping my feet on top.

"Get your feet off my fucking desk, gargoyle."

"No, I need to be comfortable for what I'm about to say, and I need you to listen to what I have to say so we can get this out the way. During our little fight yesterday, after we left, the queen was turned to stone and hit by a car, so she's dead—"

"And the king?"

"Alive and well, but when we returned to the realm I

learned of a dangerous secret, I guess you can say, that when one of the royals die, their line goes with them. All of the queen's family is dropping dead or falling ill, and the only way to preserve the future lines is for a new king and queen to arise. Now—"

"You don't even have to ask. I'll be more than happy to assume the position."

"I bet you will. You were always a little on the funny side, but that's not what I meant. I know what the king and queen promised you, your clan, but the agreement was verbal, never written. Realistically, as the only "child" if that can even be said, that the queen and king have, it is my job and duty to take over the kingdom. Now, initially, I wasn't going to, and I'm not sure if it is something I even want to have immediate effect, as you know, Pandora is my true mate, and I'll have to have the mating ceremony and then the coronation, but one thing I would like to give to you is the position in which I have, the kingdom's protector. I know for a fact you can protect us. I'd like to offer you and your clan safe passage into our realm and a living situation there as well. I think we'd be better off working together, then apart."

I waited for Black to answer me. As I sat across from him, his nostrils flared as if he was smelling something. He turned his head to the side, and his face changed.

"What's the problem?"

"You smell like Luna, why?"

"Is that any of your business?"

"It is. She's my employee, and of course, it's against the rules to...to do whatever you're thinking."

"Funny you're talking about following rules since you've broken one of the biggest ones by staying in the human world. You've been here what, about a year or so? Luna is your employee, so you shouldn't be worried about her personal business, should you?"

Black jumped up from his seat and slammed his fists on the desk, sending them straight through the top of it. I stood up from my seat, pushing it back, figuring we were about to go another round in his office. The last time I was here, the queen was alive, and if I didn't know any better, I'd say her essence was still surrounding me.

"You're so mad, but why? She's just your employee, what would there be to be so upset about?"

"She's more than just my employee, and you know it."

"Not until this very moment. I knew you liked her, but damn, I think you might be in love, Stone."

His fists were stuck in the holes of his desk, and I couldn't do anything but laugh because I knew the arousal between us caused our scents to mix together and become one.

"Black, relax, I have it on good authority that she doesn't want you, so you might as well just let this one go, man. Besides, you'll never break the secret and let her know what we are because you're more loyal than that."

"Am I? Try me!"

"If you want the position, and I know you do, you'll mind your manners and keep the secret and hold it dear. As the protector, that's your job to keep the kingdom safe by any means necessary. Eventually, you'll have to close your little bar down."

"Who said I was going to ACCEPT!" he yelled as he pulled out his fists and ran towards me. I moved out of the way, and Black ran straight into the door.

"Stone, I was promised something, and I want the happiness of my people!"

"Yes, we all want the happiness of our people, and I want the longevity of it. If I don't get on the throne, or at least become the elect, there's no telling how many people will die. Just think about it like this, I have no bloodline, no one to die if indeed I do go on, at least not yet. Help me save our people, and let's stop the fighting. I'm not going to fight you over a woman, and I'm done fighting over a kingdom and people who are the same as us."

"No, my gargoyle, we are not the same. You were created, something like a monster. I am a thorough—"

"No, you're not. All of you are hybrids, a watered down version! Now, I'm done fucking asking you to play nice! Either play nice, or don't, but I guarantee, you don't want to go to war with me; that's a bet."

I pushed him out of the way and opened the door. Heading back out into the bar. I wanted to tell Luna goodbye but now wasn't the damn time. I needed to get back into the realm and figure out what to do next.

I didn't want to be with Pandora, that was something I had already made clear, but surely, there was going to have to be something I could do. If I even became the elect, I hoped that would stop my people from dying, because after spending time with Luna, I realized I don't want to be miserable just because of tradition. I was created outside of what tradition says, so why should I be bound to the same customs as the rest of the people? Why should they be? We should be able to live freely and happily.

I rushed out of the bar heading toward the portal back to the realm. I would miss Luna, but if it was the last thing I did, I would be back. I would just have to figure out how she could fit into my life with me being a king, king elect, or whatever the fuck I was at this point.

❧ 18 ❧

LUNA

Stone ran right past me and out of the bar like his ass was on fire, and I didn't know what that was about. When I called out to him, he didn't answer me, so I figured he didn't ear me. I must have not been loud enough. There was so much going on in this one night, I didn't know how to take it. Pandora was beautiful, and I couldn't understand really what the problem between her and Stone was, but it wasn't my business. Then, there was Stone and Black, and I didn't know what to make of that either, so that was crazy, but right now, all I could do was focus on Stone and getting his attention. I wanted to know what was going on and when I'd hear from him again. He said he would be around, but I didn't know when, and I was starting to miss him, even with him just walking right out the front door and only being a few feet away.

"Terry, can you watch the register for me quickly? I'll be right back."

Terry was one of Black's cousins or something, the only other person I'd trust to make sure the bar was straight because Black's ass was way too lazy.

"Yeah, I got it, go ahead."

I nodded my head and ran, well, hobbled my way to chase after Stone. I wasn't and couldn't run anywhere, but that wouldn't stop me from trying to catch up to him. He was obviously moving quickly, because, for a minute, I lost sight of him until I saw him walking to the other side of the alley.

What was he doing over there?

"Stone!" I called out to him once again, but the traffic and noise around me drowned out my words. I couldn't move that quickly, but there was nowhere for him to go, so I figured even with me hobbling, I'd eventually make it to him.

As I crossed the street to get to the other side of the alleyway Stone was tucked in...well, it looked like it was becoming smaller, and then bigger. I hadn't taken my meds for the night, so I couldn't blame it on that, and even if I wanted to that wasn't going to happen, but I had to see what was going on. I kept walking closer to Stone and the wall, and then I saw him back up to the far wall and take off running. I just knew he was about to hurt himself.

"STONE!"

Though I couldn't run because of the pain I was in, or I shouldn't have been able to, something inside of me made it possible. I don't know if it was the fear of what might happen to him from hitting the wall or what, but I took off running after him, praying he wasn't hurt.

"Stone, Stone!" I yelled as I approached, but when I got to the spot he should've been in, there was nothing there. He...he wasn't there.

"What the—" And just like that, I too was snatched through whatever hole in the wall there was, and I can't even say it was a hole because there wasn't an opening there. It was just all brick.

How the hell did I go through a brick wall and not feel anything, and where was I now?

"Mph..." I grunted as I landed on the ground, flat on my ass.

From above me, a hand reached out to me, trying to help me up.

"Stone, what the hell is going on? Where are we?"

🦋 19 🦋

STONE

Of course, I could hear Luna calling me, but I just knew that she wasn't going to cross the street. She was supposed to be at work. I had never felt so conflicted in my life. I had so many emotions going through my body. Why was I trying so hard to make everyone else happy but myself? If I was king, surely, I could do anything I wanted, and I knew with everything inside me that Pandora wasn't my true mate, so I was supposed to be miserable for the sake of a kingdom? That made no sense. Then, to find out that Black, whether he wanted to admit it or not, was madly in love with Luna, that did something to me. It had only been a day, but I was more than just attracted to her, I was attached to her. If I stayed in the realm, I would never see her again, but there was something different about her, and I knew it. There was only one person who could give me the answers I sought, and that was Jonas, so when I heard her calling out to me, I assumed she'd stay near the bar since she was supposed to be working, but here she was, crossing the road. I assumed I could make it back inside of the realm without her noticing, but that was just stupid to believe, because as I was running toward the wall, it was too late for me to stop running, or I probably would have hurt myself, so I had to go inside.

Once I made it through, I stayed on the other side for a moment, trying to see if I could feel her getting any closer, and I could. I could feel Luna like a hunger, an insatiable hunger. She was just...I don't know, and as she got closer to the wall, I pulled her through. No, I wasn't thinking, I was reacting. I didn't know how long I would be away from her, and this way, well, maybe I wouldn't have to. She was the most intriguing creature in all the damn universe, and I wanted her to be mine. Now, I don't give a damn if it's only been a day. In a day, she's made me feel more alive than I've ever felt, and I'd be a fool to leave her not knowing where this could go or without least seeing where it was going.

"Where are we, Stone?" she asked me, looking up at me innocently.

"We're in my home. Here, stand up." I pulled her up with one hand and onto her feet.

"Ho—home? What the fuck are you talking about, Stone? I just saw you walk through a wall. I just walked through a wall. Did you slip me something?"

"How would I have done that? With my tongue?
Come on, follow me."

"No, I'm not following you until you explain some things to me. Where are we?"

"Do you trust me, Luna?" She had her head held down, and I lifted her chin with my finger.

"I did, strangely. Now, I don't know if I should. Some crazy shit is going on, and I don't know how to feel about it."

"Trust me, and I promise, you'll understand, and if you're still uncertain or afraid, I'll take you back myself, and you'll never hear from me again."

I wanted to give her a choice, but if I waited too long, she wouldn't make a choice, so I walked ahead of her. I was her only way back anyway, so she'd have to go with me or be left behind.

"Wait for me, Stone!" she said with an attitude. I knew if I got too far away from her she'd want to catch up.

I turned around and held out my hand, and she accepted it almost instinctively.

For the first few minutes, we were quiet. I wasn't sure of what to say, but every few minutes, I heard her take a deep breath, amazed at what I assumed was the palace and the landscape. It would surprise anyone. Even sometimes I was still in shock at its true beauty, not to mention the other houses that surrounded it and how it was laid out in white stones for a walkway.

"Look up there." I pointed to the top of the palace.

"What am I looking for, exactly? I can't see that well."

"The statues...look at the statues."

She looked up and scanned the sky, looking at the statues that aligned the top of the palace.

"What about them? They look like gargoyles."

"Four queens and four kings, all to represent the four corners of the realm."

"The what? And there's one above them.... who is that supposed to be?" She squinted her eyes tightly, trying to see what I was showing her.

"A long time ago, centuries and centuries ago, the magical community was being attacked by several great evils, one of which was humans. In order to defeat their enemies, the king of the magical community, Kairas and his mother, Florence, gave birth to a son who could unite the communities by marrying a fairy princess. King Kairo, was born of love and of course, magic. His mother and father were royalty in their rights, but an alliance was what they were missing. King Kairo and Queen Zaya reigned for a very long time, with the other kings and queens in the other corners of the realm, but when the gargoyles, which of course are all sorts of breeds, started mating and mixing with humans and other creatures, war struck out. Someone's always trying to be on top, and in the middle of a great battle, King Kairo and Queen Zaya had their trusted shaman, Jonas create a weapon so great, it would defeat all who came against them."

"What was the weapon?" Luna asked as if it were story time.

"It was a pure gargoyle, the first of its kind, and when he defeated the enemy of 1250 AD, he was named the kingdom's protector. He could do that best from the highest peak of the kingdom, thus watching over them for eternity, and he still does."

"Stone...this is a lot. I don't know what you're saying. I feel like I'm dreaming like you're talking crazy."

"You think I'm talking crazy, but I'm being honest. The overseer, the protector, is me, Luna. Look up there, and then look at me."

Luna looked again, and then back at me, and she did that a few times until it finally sunk in, and she began backing up.

"Sto—Stone, I...I don't understand, that would make you—"

"An immortal, or damn near close. Don't be afraid. I would never hurt you, I promise."

She folded her arms and scrunched up her nose. "I didn't say you would hurt me, Stone. I'm just trying to understand. So, you're saying you're a gargoyle? I thought you all sit on buildings and things...please explain this to me."

We continued walking, and I gave her the rundown about how gargoyles were cursed, but how in the realm, we weren't and were free to live. I also had to explain to her the situation about Black and myself, Pandora, and a few other things that she'd need to know whether she was here or working in Black's bar forever, which I hoped she wouldn't.

"I... I think I need to sit down, Stone. This is a bit, overwhelming."

"I can only imagine, here, sit down."

I helped her take a seat in the golden bench in front of the palace. Only royalty was allowed to sit on it, but I'd sat on it a few times, and to me, Luna was more than royalty—she was better than that.

"So, if this is supposed to be some kind of like, secret place, why would you bring me here? Why would you pull me through the fold?"

"Because, there are a few things I need explained to me, and I figured it would be better if you were here, so Jonas could help us both understand."

"Us both? Understand what, Stone?"

The bun her hair was in was now flopping and dropping over the top of her forehead. I pushed the dreads that were falling in her face behind her and rubbed her face. She swooned under my touch.

"I know you feel it too. I can feel what you feel. The first night I met you, I knew you were carrying a lot of pain because I felt the pain too. It was inside of me like it's inside of you. Now, Pandora was chosen as my true mate, but something about that doesn't seem right to me. I can feel Pandora too but in a different way. I can almost hear her thoughts, but there's no connection there...we have nothing between us. Since I'm different than the other gargoyles, I wonder if it's possible for my true mate to be someone else, to be someone other than a gargoyle."

Before I could continue, one of the gargoyles from the protection detail was running my way. I quickly stood up and in front of Luna. I knew how some of the old heads could be, especially about humans.

"Stone, Jonas said he needs to speak with you right away, and it's very urgent."

"Where is he?"

"He's with the king, you must hurry."

There was no way I was going to make it to his room fast enough with Luna unless we flew. I felt bad because I was going to rip out of these clothes, at least my shirt, and I didn't know how Luna was going to take to the wings.

"What's going on, Stone? What's the problem?"

"We need to get to the king's room, quickly, and the only way to do that is to fly."

"Fly? Oh, hell no, Luna doesn't fly. I've never even been on a plane before."

"This is much safer, I promise, you just gotta trust me."

She shook her head no, but I nodded my head yes. She didn't have a choice because there was no way I was going to leave her down here on the ground like this. I grabbed her by her hand, and my wings tore through the shirt, showing their ash color immediately.

"Stone," she whispered as she began touching their rough exterior. "They're beautiful, Stone."

"Not as beautiful as you." I closed my arms around her and soared through the air. I knew if too much air got into her lungs, she'd die, so I held her as tightly to my chest as possible. Though she couldn't see the sky as well as she'd probably like, I could feel the thankfulness and... perhaps blessing she felt by being able to experience something like this.

Finally, we made it to the window of the king's room, and I didn't have time to think or time to wonder if she was going to be received well, because at the end of the day, this was now about to be my damn kingdom, and even the old king would have to agree to the terms of the new king, I didn't give a damn how it went down.

"What's going on, Stone?" she asked once we landed.

"I need to check on a few things. Jonas, the shaman, has requested me, and honestly, I need to see him as well, but don't worry."

"Oh, I'm not worried. I know you'll take care of me."

"More than you know. Come on in here with me."

I pulled her into the room, and all eyes were on us. What the guard failed to tell me was that not only was Jonas and the King in here but so was Pandora.

"Jonas, my king, what seems to be the trouble?"

Jonas looked around my body, trying to scope out Luna, and I held her behind me. I felt ridiculously protective over her and would hate to see what I would do to my kind for fucking with her.

"What did you do? How could you bring her here, to our home?" Pandora took several steps toward us, pointing at her.

"Back the fuck up, Pandora. Luna is here because I brought her here, and we need to speak to Jonas alone. I have a question for him, and it doesn't concern you. In the meantime, what seems to be so urgent that I had to rush up here?"

The king cleared his throat and stepped forward and shook his head. "I think I might know what is happening now...It seems as if things are finally back in order around here. The queen's people who were ill and on the brink of death, are no longer sick and seem to be fine. What did you do? You spoke with Black I assume, but you didn't complete the true mate bond, so what is going on? Jonas, do you have any answers?"

Jonas was a man of normal brooding, and he was about to pick it up right now. He wore a troublesome look on his face, and I just knew whatever he was going to say, it was going to be bad.

"Well, Jonas, what is it? Damn, don't make that face, spit it out!" I yelled, and I could see Pandora's face without even looking at her. She looked like her head was going to pop off of her shoulders.

"My king, might I speak with Stone and his friend alone, please?"

"Alone? Does this not concern me and my kingdom? Why should I leave?"

"My king, I mean no disrespect in saying this, but will he not soon be king? Will you not be going into retirement? Pandora, should you not be helping the king arrange for the queen's funeral?"

Pandora stared us down, and I could almost tell she was plotting an attack against Luna, but my eyes glowed at her, letting her know that if she brought her ass this way, she would be dealt with, period, and she quickly changed her attitude.

"King Kairo, perhaps Jonas is right. Since you've made the announcement in our absence, there is no need to speak on it again. For a queen as great as Zaya, she deserves a long cele-bration, and it's a long, beautiful celebration she shall have."

"Yes, and then, after she's buried, I will be joining her in the afterlife, one way or another."

I didn't even know what to say to that. I wasn't going to argue with someone who wanted to move on to the afterlife. He loved Zaya so much, I could only imagine how he felt, and I prayed I never had to. Pandora gave me a daring, threat-ening look before leaving the room with the king, and I knew somehow, this shit was far from over.

20

JONAS

For years, I had wondered when the differences of Stone's conception would either cause a problem, or change things as we knew it, and now, both had happened. If I wasn't mistaken, and there was only one way to check, we'd been doing things entirely wrong. Things had become disastrous, and I needed to perform a few acts to make sure before it came down the pipeline.

When the king and Pandora left, I waited for the door to close completely before I spoke. Gargoyles have amazing hearing, and even with the door closed, we would need to whisper.

"Stone, introduce me to your lovely friend, please."

He looked at me, trying to read if it was ok to step aside, and I let him know it was by standing back. I didn't want him to think I was trying to hurt her, because I wasn't.

"Jonas, this is Luna, Luna, this is the Shaman, Jonas."

"The one that created you?" she asked as she looked deep into his eyes.

"Yes, with a little help from the king and queen.

It's nice to meet you, my child."

I reached for her hand, and Stone's eyes were on us the entire time. When I touched her hand, I had a vision so great, so scary, it would turn this kingdom upside down, but it didn't negate the fact that I still needed to run some tests to see if this was their feelings projecting onto me, or if this was real.

"Jonas, is everything ok?" Stone asked, his eyebrows furrowed.

"I believe everything might be ok. If you'll both allow me, I'd like to run a few tests. I'm sure the question you want to ask me is a question I'm already trying to answer."

"Let me ask it anyway just so I can get it out. Could someone else be my true mate and not Pandora? From the books I've read, and from watching Zaya and Kairo, even Quamir and Luciana, the cooks, I can tell what the bond should look like, and I don't have that with Pandora, but I know something is happening or has happened between Luna and I, and I'd like to know if it's possible, for a human to be my true mate."

I dared not to admit it aloud, but it was a possibility anytime magic was involved. The universe has a way of keeping and making each world balanced, whether it be human or magical.

"Well, I'd like to run a few tests to see how your blood reacts. We once ran a test with your blood and Pandora's, and they immediately reacted, but after twenty minutes, the blood separated. Zaya and Kairo were so certain that the two of you were meant to be, they just decided it would be, but truthfully, Pandora has never been your true mate, and if you would have completed the mating ritual, I'm not so sure it would have been successful. I think it would have failed, honestly."

Stone was now holding Luna's hand, smiling.

"What does all of this mean, Stone? I'm so damn confused right now."

"No more confused than me. You know what it's like for me to go my whole life thinking one thing, but knowing it probably wasn't right, to now, this? I mean, nobody's happier about it than I am, but this, this is just...it's fucked up. So, how do we do this blood test? Is it going to be the same as the one previously?"

"Blood test? Wait a minute, I'm not gon' get my blood sucked or nothin', right?"

Stone and I both looked at Luna wondering if we misheard her.

"We ain't vampires, Luna, we're gargoyles. Ain't no blood-suckin' goin' on around here."

"Exactly. I'll prick your finger and gather a few drops, no more than five and see what happens between them. If the blood mixes and stays mixed, then it potentially means.... well, that Luna could be your true mate. If not, then, at least you'll know."

Stone brought Luna closer to him and held her.

"What do you think? Is this something you want to do?"

"I don't know, Stone. All of this is a bit overwhelming. I mean, it hasn't been any downtime since we've been here. I don't know what I should be thinking or how I should be feeling, and what about Black? He's gonna fuckin' kill me for missing this much of my shift."

"No, he won't. He's a gargoyle too, and he understands gargoyle business, but since he's in love with you, he may be a bit jealous. I wouldn't worry about losing your job though; if anything, he's going to want to keep you as close to him as he possibly can."

"If it will make it any easier on you, you don't have to leave right away. Perhaps you could stay for a bit to feel things out and see what our world is like. That way, if the two of you do wind up being true mates, none of this will seem foreign to you. You will already be comfortable." I offered a valuable solution. I knew already in my heart and through the vision I had of her, she was, in fact, his true mate, but this road would not be easy, and it was one that couldn't be forced upon either of them. They would have to choose this life. For years, we had been making the choices for everyone else, perhaps it was time to let things happen since they would happen no matter what. With a more genuine bond, it could lead to a much happier rule, because one day, she would indeed become the queen of all gargoyles.

"I don't have any clothes my phone isn't even here. Where would I sleep?" Luna asked, looking directly at Stone.

"You don't need clothes; we can have someone bring you a wardrobe for your time here. Your phone wouldn't work here anyway, so you don't need it, and you can sleep in one of the suites, of course."

"Alone?"

"Not if you don't want to," Stone said genuinely, making Luna's face blush with redness.

"Well, I guess you've solved all of my problems I would have. If all of those things are worked out, I can't imagine why I shouldn't stay."

"Neither can I. Now, Stone, may I have a few drops of your blood so that we can begin the test?"

"Luna, will you do this for me? You told me I should do what I want, and this is what I want. I'd like to make sure I'm not crazy, not that I need some test to tell me what I feel. I don't, but it would be nice to know if it was already written for us."

Hesitantly, Luna held out her hand. "Go ahead and stick me before I change my mind, please."

I knew she would do it, but it was nice that everything was falling into place. I grabbed my blade, the one I used for special spells as such and pulled Luna over to the caldron. Her hand hovered over the cauldron steadily as I quickly sliced it open and allowed her blood to flow into the side of it.

"Mmm...that stings."

"Yes, I know. Here, let me help you with that."

I placed my hand over hers, and the wound that was bleeding healed itself, stitching her skin back together. She smiled and tilted her hand left to right, checking to see if this was some sort of magic trick, which in a way, it was. I am a shaman after all.

Next, Stone stepped forward and placed his hand over the cauldron, repeating the same steps I had before, and his blood was a much deeper, darker red than Luna's, that of a gargoyle's. It was truly a sight to see. I whispered a prayer up to the gargoyle ancestors who watched over us and let the blood do its thing.

"What now? I mean, is there anything else I need to do?"

"No, Luna, now, Stone can show you around the kingdom and get you more acquainted with everything."

I bowed to Stone and the future queen and let them walk toward the door, but before I did, I grabbed Luna's wrist and pulled her back.

"It's ok, Stone, go ahead. Give me a second," she said to Stone as he was ready to jump into the only mode he knew, defense.

"Is there something wrong, Jonas?"

"No, no, that's what I wanted to tell you. It isn't my place, but I feel like I should say it anyway. Your womb is not shut, and you won't feel that pain between your legs you've been feeling. You've been healed. The moment you stepped into the realm, you were made whole again."

"Whole again?"

"Yes, it will be as if it never happened. Your body will no

longer suffer the effects of the miscarriage. I'm saying this to say; I can feel the...uh.... tension between you and Stone. The wonderful thing about magic is it can fix almost everything. Not only did I heal your hand, but I've healed you completely, well, physically."

"How...how did you know?" she whispered.

"I see the things people don't want me to see.

Gargoyle bless you, now go, and enjoy your time here."

Tears welled up in her eyes as she walked away, and I knew the road ahead would be rocky, but it would be well worth it for my people.

21

BLACK

I was so mad, I could have killed Stone's ass. He was so arrogant and thought he was the best gargoyle to have ever lived, and that couldn't have been farther from the truth. The mere fact that he was able to read me on how I felt about Luna had me fucked up. It was true, I was madly in love with her, and I didn't know how to act around her. She wasn't like most of the human women I had come in contact with, and I knew many of them. I missed work the night before, so I could go and get my rocks off, and it wasn't enough; it never would be until I had Luna. She was everything I could ever dream of, and there was nothing like her in the gargoyle world, and I knew it.

Angrily stumbling out of my office, I went into the front of the bar to see how she was doing. I wanted to see where her head was at and if she was feeling Stone. If she could like him, she could like me, because we come from the same place, the same thing, same situation pretty much. Now, I know what you're thinking—I'm not Stone, and he's not me, but we weren't that different, not enough to where she couldn't choose me.

When I got behind the bar, Terry was serving and ringing up the customers.

"Terry, where's Luna?"

"She said she had to go outside and get somethin', so I'm covering for her till she gets back." "When was that?

"Shit, it's been about an hour...maybe she's still outside or something. You know it be hot in here to humans, and she did have that procedure."

I just shook my head at this gargoyle. She was gone for an hour, and he didn't think to tell me or go and get her? What the fuck? I went outside to check to see if I saw her, and when I didn't, I started to panic. I didn't know where she might've gone off to, but I could smell her scent, so she couldn't have gone too far. At least I didn't think so till I followed her scent all the way to the other side of the alley where it was strongest. I hoped nothing bad happened to her, but I couldn't be sure. When I got to the end, I sniffed around some more, trying to smell her, and then the trail seemed to pick up again at the barrier. I thought I was going crazy. There was no way she was in the realm; would have Stone taken her in there? That was something I just found hard to believe, and if I did go inside, I would be seen as an enemy because the Scovel clan had never been welcomed due to all the war and battles we'd had, but if something bad happened to Luna, I wouldn't even know, and there was only one way for me to know. Terry could handle the bar, and he knew what to do in my absence. There was no way I was going back to tell him I had to dip off.

It had been a long time since I stepped foot in the realm, but I was about to do it to make sure she was ok. I knew Stone wouldn't hurt her, but anything could happen to her if she weren't with Stone. Our people didn't take too kindly to humans and not them being in the realm. I stepped back to gain momentum and ran straight through. As soon as I entered, I instantly felt like I made a mistake because of all the gargoyles who were standing guard trying to watch me.

"Black, what are you doing here?" one of the guards asked me.

"I don't want any trouble, I'm looking for Stone. Is he here?"

"What do you want with him? You say you don't want trouble, but it seems like you've come seeking it out."

These fools were gon' make me flip out. I know in the past I've been ruthless and didn't give a fuck, but that's not what this was.

"Look, I just came here to see him because we have some business we need to discuss. Is he here or not?"

I was about to growl, but I needed to keep my cool because if I didn't, a fight would break out, and I was outnumbered.

Before any of us could react, from the sky, I saw those pretentious ash wings flapping toward me. It was Stone. When he landed, it was always so smooth, like he was just the shit. I hated this man with everything in me.

"Black, what are you doing here?"

"Where's Luna? Is she ok?" I hurriedly asked, getting straight to the point.

"She's fine. She's in a suite taking a shower."

"A shower? Why is she here? Why would you bring her here?"

"Why are you worried about it? It has absolutely nothing to do with you. Besides, she has no feelings for you, and if I'm right, she's my true mate, and you know how that goes. I'll stop at nothing to defend that bond, so you need to leave and get on with your business, man."

"True mate? That could never happen. A human, a true mate, for you? Ain't no fuckin wa—"

"Hear ye, hear ye, King Kairo has made a royal decree

that in a day's time, we will begin the celebration of the homegoing of Queen Zaya. Invitations will follow this evening."

Everyone turned around to see the royal announcer with a giant scroll in his hand. I hated this old school shit. It was 2018, and it was time we started living like it.

When he was gone, I looked at Stone, and Pandora was in both of our faces.

"Did you say, true mate? Luna is whose true mate, Black's?"

It was then that I saw my way out. Everyone in the realm or otherwise knew Pandora was Stone's true mate, or she was supposed to be. I wanted Luna for myself, to possess her, to be mine, and if Stone was in the way, I couldn't have her, but Pandora...she was a spitfire, and she would help me get him out of the way.

"She's my true mate, Pandora. As a matter of fact, I'm getting my things out of our suite tonight. I don't want to lead you on in any kind of way, not at all," Stone said with authority in his voice, but with all that bass, it still wasn't doin' shit. Pandora wasn't about to go for that.

She pulled him out of earshot, and I knew it was about to go down. She must have forgotten though, we all had super hearing, and I could hear them even if they weren't near me, but I didn't give a shit about what she was about to say to him. All I cared about was getting to Luna and talking to her myself. I knew she wasn't going to know anything about this true mate shit, at least not understanding it completely, and if she was going to be anybody's true mate, it was going to be mine.

When they walked away, I waited until they got far enough away, and I used that as a distraction to let me escape so that I could find Luna myself.

22

PANDORA

"Get your fucking hands off me, Stone! Stop, stop!"

I couldn't believe my ears, and my heart felt like it was breaking. I wish I could say confusion was the only way I was feeling.

"You've known her for what, a day or so? She's human! She will die, and you will be left alone! Why not just be happy with me, someone who already loves you. Somebody who wants to be with you and can be with you for centuries on end? I'm a princess for gargoyle sake!"

He looked at me like I had a flesh-eating disease like I was the most disgusting thing in the world to him.

"Pandora, do you hear yourself? If it wasn't for her, we would be together and be miserable. Why would you want to be with someone who can't truly love you? Someone who doesn't see you that way? You've been good to me, and I'm sorry I let it get this far, but this, between me and you, it's been over, forever. It never truly started."

"Never truly started? You weren't saying that all those nights we were in bed together making love!"

"Making love? No, we were fucking, that's it, that's all.

Pandora, listen to me, you're a good catch, and any gargoyle would be glad and lucky to have you."

"Just not you, huh? I'm just not the one for you, is that right? What are you going to do when she dies? When she's too old to be with you? What will happen when she dies during childbirth if you get her pregnant? What about me and our child?"

"What child?"

I didn't mean to say that. It was a spur of the moment decision to say to make him stay and be with me, but I didn't know what else to do.

"I know you're lying, Pandora. You would try to trap me just to keep me? See, that's why I don't even want to be with you. If I were you, I'd get it together, Pan before you ruin the friendship we got over some stupid jealousy. I gotta go. I need to get back to Luna. I'll get my stuff when you're not in there, so you don't have to deal with it."

I didn't even get to say another word. He flew away from me and backed up to the palace. I wanted to chase after him, to rewind time and make it so that I didn't say that, but damn it, it was too late for all of that now, and I might have ruined my one chance at happiness unless I could sabotage their "relationship". She wouldn't even know what to do with a gargoyle, no less Stone. She couldn't fuck him like I could or protect him like I could. She had to go, and I would make it so.

❧ 23 ❧

LUNA

I have never in my life had a shower that amazing before. Like, it went beyond being clean and crossed straight into being fucking amazing. The water was perfect and hot, and it was big as hell! It had so much room in it. A bitch like me had only seen shit like this in a hotel or a movie.

After everything I found out today, I was kind of worn out, but it made so much sense now. Like, the reason why Black didn't allow me in the bar at a certain time, or even why he seemed super strong, and sometimes why I thought his eyes changed colors when he was angry, something Stone made me aware of. His wings...God, they were beautiful; he was beautiful. He reminded me of a stone angel, but I tried not to think like that because this was magic, not religion, but it was hard not to think like that.

Then what Jonas told me fucked me up. I wasn't hurting, which was true, and I hadn't been bleeding since I got here. I didn't feel weak; if anything, I felt stronger than I ever had.

When I came out of the shower, there were clothes waiting for me, and I wondered where they came from. I was so amazed by how everything around here operated. They still had a TV to watch, even though there was no cell reception, that's what I didn't understand, but who needs a phone when you have no one to talk to? Who the fuck was I going to tell about this shit? I couldn't. I promised to keep his secret, and I would do so until the end of time, well, my time.

Hearing that you're someone's true mate is a crazy thing. I believed in love at first sight, but everything was moving so quickly, I didn't know how to feel. I was attracted to Stone, and there was something there, but I didn't know how I was supposed to go about even agreeing to something like this. I mean, dating was one thing, but Stone was practically royalty. He would be crowned king from what I was hearing, and this gargoyle nation didn't need some ghetto ass chick like me from Louisville ruling over a world I knew absolutely nothing about.

Going over to the clothes, I dropped the white plush towel I had and picked up the bra and panty set someone had hand selected for me. This was the work of a woman because it was no way a man could have known my size. I just wanted to thank whoever did this for me, because this shit was crazy.

I was about to put the bra on when the door to the suite flew open. I quickly grabbed the towel and wrapped it around me, jumping behind the bed as to hide my body.

"Oh, shit, Luna, I'm sorry. I didn't mean to barge in. I figured you'd be dressed by now or still in the shower. I'll leave and give you some..."

"No, Stone...don't leave."

What was I saying? Why was I saying that? When I was around him, I never wanted him out of my presence, never.

"Are you ok? Do you need something?" he asked, stepping toward my direction.

"I need you," I whispered. I was talking crazy. It was like I couldn't control my thoughts or my own words.

"What did you say?" He was now directly in front of me, just inches away.

I know I shouldn't have been thinking like this, but I was desperate to feel what it would be like to make love to Stone because that's exactly what it would be. I knew it wouldn't be some random fuck, and since Jonas said I was healed down there, what would be the harm in it? I wanted it just as badly as he did. I could feel it when we kissed when I was in his arms. We wanted each other, and it seemed like now, he was panting in front of me.

"I said, I. NEED. YOU." I dropped my towel and stepped closer to him, closing the gap between us. My naked body against him.

"Luna...don't tempt me. I'll take you right here, but I don't want to hurt you."

"Maybe I want to be hurt..."

That was all it took for us to get started. I knew it would hurt, but feel so good at the same time.

Stone took off his shirt that was ripped at the back where his wings were, and his body was as chiseled as I knew it would be. His stomach was like a washboard. He looked like he'd been handcrafted from the finest stone in the world. His pants hung from his hips, showing his v-cut waist, and I wanted to close my eyes before I saw what was next. I felt his dick when I was pressed up against him earlier, but I knew feeling it and seeing it would be two totally different things. His shoes seemed to have magically disappeared, I didn't know where they went, and then, his pants came off, and it was like staring into the face of the heavens. His dick was so big, so thick, so long. If I had stitches, he would've ripped them. Healed or not, I started to get nervous.

Stone wrapped his arms around my waist and pulled me as closely to him as he could. His hips were perfectly aligned with my stomach, and his dick was pulsing against my vagina, begging to go inside.

"Don't be nervous, Luna. Imma take care of you, baby."

I looked away, and he pulled my face back to look at him.

"Don't hide that beautiful face. Look me in the eyes. I don't want you to miss any of this."

My eyes almost popped out of my head when he said that. He picked me up in his strong arms and carried me to the bed, lightly dropping me onto the covers, making me giggle. I felt like a teenager who was about to lose their virginity.

When his fingertips started going up my thigh, my pussy started tingling in ways that I didn't even know was possible. I had never been so aroused so easily. Just when I thought this was about to be some sweet make love type of shit, it changed drastically. He pried my legs open and stared directly into my pussy, like it was a mirror like he could see himself inside of it.

My hands flew up to my mouth because I was already about to let out a moan, but I didn't want to embarrass myself. I was so worked up, my body started squirming, and he hadn't even put his tongue on me yet. I thought about that too soon, because his tongue started easing its way up my right leg, and then when he got to my pussy, he opened her up big and wide, stretching my lips, and I felt like he was eating a full course meal. His lips explored the folds of my pussy like never before. I moaned and writhed with pleasure, trying not to be too loud.

"Ughn, Stone..."

"Shh...Luna just lay back, and enjoy it."

And enjoy it I was. His tongue was doing circles around my clit, flicking and licking back and forth. My pussy was swelling with cum, and I just prayed I didn't explode all over his face, even though the way he was licking, it seemed like that was what he wanted.

It started to feel so good, I tried to shut my legs on his head, but every time I did, he just pushed them open more.

"Mmm...you're being a bad girl, Luna. You like the way I'm punishing this little pussy?"

When he asked me that, I couldn't hold back anymore. I didn't want to just turn into a beast like that, but I couldn't help it. He was bringing it out of me. I curled my legs around his neck, and he knew what I wanted because he flipped me over, and I was now on his face, bouncing up and down like a pogo stick. One of his hands was on my ass, and the other was on my breast, squeezing my nipple just enough to hurt but to also bring pleasure.

"Stone!" I screamed. I was about to cum. I needed the release something awful!

I looked down and watched him eat my pussy, and it was amazing. His eyes were wide open, watching me watch him, and that made it even worse. Finally, I let go, feeling free, and released myself all over his face, wetting him and myself up.

I was going to get up and clean myself, but that was not about to happen. When I climbed off of his face, he picked me up above his body and sat me right on his dick. Thank God he gave me head first, or I could've died from his length. I could feel that shit in my throat. I wondered how he was able to get his dick sucked without choking a bitch to death because I was choking from the pussy.

"Shit, Luna! Damn!" he moaned as I did my best to ride him. It was feeling so good, but I couldn't keep up with him. I had never had a dick this big before. His hands were around my waist, steadily holding me, and it felt so damn good.

"Stone, I'm..."

"Uhn-uhn, not yet!"

Suddenly, we were off the bed, and in the air. His beautiful wings flew out, lifting us into the air. I was riding him in the fucking air!

"You trust me?" he asked me, looking directly in my eyes.

"Of course, yes!"

At this point, I would have agreed to anything, but I was about to get more than I bargained for. With his wings still flapping, and us still in the air, we flew to the wall, where his back was against it, and I was on top of him, and I was no longer doing the work. He was sliding in and out of me, bouncing me on his dick. His dick was crashing into my pussy like waves along the beach, and then, the unexpected happened. He slid his finger into my ass. Normally, I would not be going, but that only heightened my feelings.

This man was multi-talented. My head fell backwards, and I closed my eyes, I was starting to get motion sickness, but this was the best damn ride I'd ever had.

"Open your eyes and look at me, Luna. I want you to see me."

Shit, how could I say no? We were both close to cumming, I could tell. Shit, I had cum at least three times while his dick was inside of me. For a second, he was going so hard and so fast, I knew he was about to reach his peak, and when he did, his eyes flashed a silver-gray color, almost the same color as his wings, and I was mesmerized. He released such a loud growl that shit only turned me on more, and I didn't know how we were going to stop. The growl reverberated through my whole body, and I didn't want this to end.

"LUNA!" he said my name in a low, guttural tone, but it was so loud, it shook the whole damn room. Literally, the walls shook. Talk about making your love come down. I was so weak from getting fucked like that, I couldn't even stand up any longer. My legs fell from around his waist, but he didn't let me slip, and I knew I wouldn't. He wrapped his arms around me and flew us to the large printed rug on the floor and laid me down.

I was nervous to say anything. I didn't know if I should or

if he would speak first, but either way, this was the most perfect moment I'd ever had in my life.

After he lay me down, he walked over to the chair closest to the window, his ass cheeks glistening with juice, and when he came back, he had a blanket in his arms.

"Here, let me cover you up."

I couldn't even speak, I just nodded my head as he gently placed the blanket over me and then slid underneath, putting his arm underneath my head so that I could rest it on his chest.

"So, how do you feel?"

I couldn't stand to look him in the eyes right now, especially since they were still glowing, at least they were when he brought the blanket over.

"I feel...I feel good. I feel...amazing, Stone. This was amazing."

"You're amazing, Luna. You changed my life."

"By giving you some pussy?"

"Ha! No, by being in my life and telling me what I needed to hear and just being here. I'm surprised you haven't run away yet."

"Why would I? We're true mates, aren't we?"

He lifted my chin and snuggled his nose against mine.

"I'm yours, and you are mine, especially now. I'll kill you if you try to give that away, Luna."

My whole body shivered when he said that. He didn't have to worry; I wasn't going to give anyone what was his ever because I knew without the shadow of a doubt that nobody was ever going to love on me like he did, nobody.

We lay there for a few more minutes, and then there was a knock at the door.

"Just a minute, one second!" Stone yelled from the rug. He grabbed his pants and slid them back on, and I could see the marks from where his wings receded. I hadn't noticed till this moment as well, but he had all of these tattoos all over his body. I hadn't noticed them before, but they were so intricate and detailed. Shit, I needed his artist.

Stone went to the door and slightly opened it, pulling it open just enough for him to see who it was.

"Your presence has been requested with the king, you and the human." I heard the gargoyle say with a little attitude in his voice. I figured this was going to be a problem that we would face often. The fact that I was a human probably wouldn't sit well with a lot of the other gargoyles, but they'd have to get used to it, because the way Stone just wrecked my insides, I wasn't going anywhere now.

"Get up, baby, and get dressed. We need to go and see the king."

"Is everything ok?" I asked, getting up to reach for the clothes that were already laid out for me.

"I'm sure it is. You have nothing to worry about, but before we go in here, I should let you know that Black is here somewhere lurking around, no doubt looking for you."

"For me, why? What does he want?"

"He wants you, baby."

"But I don't want him, ever, not even a little bit."

"I know that, and I won't let him even think he can have you. Everything will be fine. Go ahead and put on your clothes and we'll see the king. It's probably about the queen's funeral arrangements." I hadn't thought about it till now, but I realized this was the "mother" he talked about dying, and I hadn't said anything.

"Wait, Stone, I need to say something to you."

"What is it, baby?"

"I could get used to you calling me baby, but that isn't it. I just wanted to say I'm sorry about your mother, your queen. I am, and if there's anything I can do to make this transition of losing her easier, just let me know."

It seemed like the world lifted off his shoulders when I said that. As I was putting on my clothes, he placed a kiss on my forehead, and in that moment, I felt closer to him than I ever had anyone else. It was the strangest thing. I had fallen for a fucking gargoyle, and nothing was making since nothing but the way I felt for him.

24

STONE

After putting our clothes back on, all I could think about was that moment we shared together. I wasn't even expecting it, even though I felt the tension and arousal between us, but I thought we'd wait it out a little while, or at least for as long as we could, and maybe that was as long as we could. I wanted us having sex to be on her terms and not anyone else's, not even mine. She felt so good, her body against mine. That was what I had been missing. I wasn't even thinking about Pandora, not until I saw her in the conference room with the king, along with Black and Jonas at a table.

Black looked like he wanted to jump and run up on me, and so did Pandora. Everyone in the room could tell what had just happened between us. Not only were we glowing, but as gargoyles, we had keen senses, and they could smell the passion on us and probably my sex still in between Luna's legs. I didn't want her to wash off because I wasn't ashamed, and she shouldn't be either. I was proud of the love we made, and whatever happened between us didn't need to be kept a secret. This wasn't the stone ages; being with a human wasn't the death sentence it once was, hopefully. I just hoped if she did get pregnant that it wouldn't rip her apart the way it had the humans in the past, but again, I'm different and am nothing like the other gargoyles. I never had been and never would be.

Luna and I walked in together hand in hand, and the king wore a smile on his face, though Pandora looked like she would die, and strangely, for the first time, I couldn't feel her. The way she felt was not in me anymore. I loved it.

"My king, you requested our presence?" I said as we walked up to the table.

"Yes, have a seat, you two. I'd like to have this conversation with all of you since all parties involved are present. Black, you couldn't have come at a better time."

"Shit, I beg to differ," he said, eyeing me and Luna.

"Luna, you ok?"

"Grrrr!" I snapped at him. "Don't address her. You address me, and she's just fine, as you can see. Here, baby, sit down, on this side." I pulled her chair out for her, and she smirked. I was going to have to get that under control, but when it came to her and another man, gargoyle, hell even an animal, I was going to be going crazy.

"Ok, enough of that. The two of you, put your dicks away, for now, we have business to discuss. Now, as you all know, I had a verbal agreement with the Scovel clan, and I'm sorry to have to break that, but I know Stone had this conversation with you already about what your role will be. You'll be the head of security, and Stone will be king."

"Uhm, I have a question?" Luna said raising her hand like we were in school. I thought it was cute.

"Are we letting humans speak in royal matters now?"

"Pandora, watch it!" I yelled.

"No, that's ok, baby, let her say how she feels, but if she's smart, she'll shut the fuck up. You might be a gargoyle, but

I'm a crazy ass bitch, and I'll fight you to the death. Whatever you had with Stone is over now, and for that, I am sorry. I can only imagine what it's like to love him and lose him, but your problem ain't with me, it needs to be with him."

"Now, if I may, your highness."

"You may go ahead."

"Wonderful, if Stone becomes king, what does that mean for me? Who will be his queen?"

"May I speak, my king?" Jonas asked, looking between Kairo and myself.

"Of course, go ahead."

"Well, if Stone becomes king and the two of you complete the true mating ceremony, then it would be you who rules."

"Even though I'm human?" she asked.

"We can change that, of course. If you choose, that is."

"What do you mean, if she chooses?" This was the first I'd ever heard of this, and judging by the looks on everyone's faces, I could tell it was for them as well.

"If she chooses, there are ways to make her a gargoyle, but we're far away from that, hopefully. After all, it is her choice, but the life expectancy of a human is very short, as we all know."

I nodded my head, and Luna looked shell-shocked, while Pandora wore an evil smirk on her face.

"Moving on, I will be...retiring in a sense to the afterlife to join my wife and the gargoyle ancestors, and before I do, I want to make sure everything is in order. Pandora, where are we with the rest of the plans for the queen's life celebration?" As Pandora spoke, and everyone else listened, I noticed smoke coming from the full-length mirror that rest against the wall, but I thought I was tripping until Jonas noticed it as well.

"Stone, guard the king!" Jonas yelled.

I jumped up on command, grabbing Luna and pushing her

behind me, behind the king. That's right, I would protect my woman over my king. I didn't give a damn. We all stood there, Black, Pandora, myself, and Jonas, watching, waiting to see what was to come of this smoke in the mirror. When the smoke dissipated, a figure appeared, and it shocked the shit out of us all.

"Zaya." I managed to get out. I couldn't believe my eyes.

"Jonas, could it be?" Kairo asked as he tried to push his way ahead of me.

"Give it a moment, my king, let me see," Jonas said as he got closer to the mirror.

"Jonas, it is I. Kairo, my sweet, dear Kairo. Stone, Pandora...."

Zaya's body had been restored, though she was in spirit form, and she had on her royal robes, dressed in purple and gold, dripping a regal air.

"My love...how...how is this possible?"

"Anything is possible when magic is involved, you should know this. Now, listen, I've come with a disheartening message, and I want to tell you before it's too late, so something can be done about it, and

I'm sorry, my darling, for what I'm about to say."

"What is it, sweetheart? Tell me."

We all stood there, watching and waiting.

"I couldn't be sure, that is, until now, but spirits talk more than any alive gargoyle or person you've ever met. As you know, I was raped, something I thought I'd kept a secret. I tried my hardest, but what you don't know, is before my womb closed on me, I did have a child, a male child. I gave it away, hoping you, my future husband would never find out. Do you remember when I went away with my family to visit the neighboring kingdom? While you were still courting me? I was pregnant, I had the baby, and I gave him away. I thought he was lost to me. I never tried to find him, but he seemed to stumble back into the fold, and I now know who it is. He has a right to the throne, and it's only right that he rule."

"Wait, did you say a son? You had a baby? Zaya..."

"There isn't much time left. I have to tell you who it is. All of this time, we've been fighting and fighting, and we've been looking in the wrong direction, once again. That baby...is Black. Please tell him I'm sorry, and I hope one day, you too can forgive me."

There were no more words to be said, and this couldn't have come at a worse time. Though Black was out of the queen's eyesight, he heard every word she said, and I couldn't be sure, but I saw an overflow of power in this room. Between Pandora, myself, Black, and even Kairo, there was a usurper amongst us, and I couldn't be sure if I only had to watch out for Black now, or Pandora as well.

The gargoyle kingdom would never be the same if he took hold of it, and there was no way in gargoyle hell I'd allow that to happen, even if I had to kill the "future king" myself.

TO BE CONTINUED...

COMING 10.03!

COMING 10.05

CPSIA information can be obtained
at www.ICGtesting.com
Printed in the USA
LVHW011928201118
597792LV00006B/499